KT-433-276

ISBN 1 85854 154 9
© Brimax Books Ltd 1995.
Published by Brimax Books Ltd, Newmarket, England 1995.
Printed in Dubai.

AROUND THE WORLD IN EIGHTY DAYS

ADAPTED BY

JOHN ESCOTT

ILLUSTRATED BY

KIM PALMER

Brimax · Newmarket · England

Jules Verne's *Around the World in Eighty Days* has been a well-loved classic of literature since it was first written in 1873. It follows the adventures of Phileas Fogg and his servant Passepartout as they try to travel around the world in eighty days for a bet of twenty thousand pounds.

The rescue of Aouda in India and of Passepartout from the Sioux indians are just two of the unexpected obstacles that seem sure to hinder Mr Fogg's long journey. Inspector Fix of Scotland Yard is convinced that Phileas Fogg has robbed a bank and pursues him around the world.

The marvellous illustrations along with the carefully adapted text make this a book that children will enjoy reading.

1

In the year of 1872, at number seven, Savile Row, Burlington Gardens, there lived a man called Phileas Fogg. He belonged to the Reform Club of London, and although he seemed to take care never to do anything which might attract attention, he was one of its strangest and most noticeable members.

Very little was known about him. He was certainly an Englishman, although perhaps not a Londoner. He was never seen at the Stock Exchange or the Bank, or in any of the offices in the City. No ship owned by Phileas Fogg had ever entered London docks, nor was he ever seen in the Law Courts. He was not a merchant or a farmer.

No, Phileas Fogg was a member of the Reform Club, and that was all.

Was he a rich man? Certainly, but no one knew how he had made his fortune, and Mr Fogg was the last person one could ask. He was no spendthrift, but nor was he a miser, for whenever money was needed for some worthy cause he would provide it quietly and even anonymously.

Had he travelled? It seemed likely, for whenever some place in the world was mentioned, he knew something about it. But Phileas Fogg had not left London for many years now. He was only ever seen taking the direct route between his home and his Club each day. There he read the newspapers or played his favourite card game of whist – not for the money he won (which went to charity) but for the pleasure of playing.

As far as it was known, he had no wife or children, no relatives or close friends. He lived alone except for a single servant who attended to his needs. He had lunch and dinner at the Club at fixed times, always in the same room and at the same table, and never entertained any guests. Then, on the stroke of midnight, he went home to bed.

The house in Savile Row was simple but comfortable. Because Phileas Fogg spent so much time at his Club, there was little work for his servant to do, but Phileas Fogg expected him to be punctual and regular. That very morning, the 2nd October, he had dismissed one servant for bringing shaving water that was two degrees cooler than it should have been.

At 11.30 am, he would leave for his Club. But now, sitting in his armchair, he was looking at the man who hoped to become his new servant.

"You are French?" Phileas Fogg asked.

The other man nodded. "My name is Jean Passepartout. I am an honest fellow, Monsieur, but I have had several occupations. I've been a travelling singer, a circus rider, a trapeze artist, a tightrope walker and a teacher of gymnastics. Finally, I was a fireman in Paris, but it is five years now since I left France and became a servant in England. I have heard that you lead a quiet and regular life in this house, and it's my hope that I can come and work for you."

"You come recommended," said Mr Fogg. "Now, you know my terms?"

"Yes, Monsieur."

"Good. What time is it?"

Passepartout took a large silver watch from his pocket. "Eleven twenty-four," he said.

"Your watch is slow," said Mr Fogg.

"Pardon me, Monsieur, but that is impossible."

"Your watch is four minutes slow. But it doesn't matter, so long as you know it. So, you are now in my service."

Having said this, Phileas Fogg picked up his hat, put it on his head and went out without another word.

After putting his right foot in front of his left 575 times, and his left in front of his right 576 times, he arrived at the Reform Club in Pall Mall. There he made his way to the dining room and sat down at his usual table. At 12.47 pm, after lunch, he went into the morning room and read *The Times* until 3.45 pm, then he picked up the *Standard* which he read until it was time for dinner.

At 5.40 pm, Phileas Fogg reappeared in the morning room and became engrossed in the *Morning Chronicle*. Half an hour later, he was joined by five of his usual whist partners and, as they got ready to play cards, they began to discuss the bank robbery which had taken place three days before. A robbery in which £55,000 had been stolen from the Bank of England.

"The bank can say goodbye to its money," said Andrew Stuart.

"Not at all," said Walter Ralph, who was a director of the Bank of England. "Police inspectors have been sent to all the main ports in America and Europe. The thief will find it hard to give them the slip."

"The *Morning Chronicle* describes him as educated and a gentleman," said Phileas Fogg. "No ordinary thief."

"Then the chances are in his favour," said Andrew Stuart, "for he must be a very clever fellow."

"Nonsense!" replied Walter Ralph. "Where in the world can he go?"

"I haven't the faintest idea," replied Andrew Stuart, "but the world is a big place, after all."

"It used to be," said Phileas Fogg.

"What do you mean?" said Andrew Stuart. "Has the world shrunk?"

"Of course it has," said Walter Ralph. "You can go round it ten times faster than you could a hundred years ago."

"But just because you can travel round it in three months – "

"In no more than eighty days," corrected Phileas Fogg.

"That's right, gentlemen," said John Sullivan, a banker. "Eighty days, now that the Great Indian Peninsular Railway has opened. This is how the *Morning Chronicle* works out the journey." And he wrote it down:

London to Suez by rail and steamer	7 days
Suez to Bombay by steamer	13 days
Bombay to Calcutta by rail	3 days
Calcutta to Hong Kong by steamer	13 days
Hong Kong to Yokohama by steamer	6 days

Yokohama to San Francisco by steamer	22 days
San Francisco to New York by rail	7 days
New York to London by steamer and rail	9 days
	Total 80 days

"But that doesn't allow for bad weather, shipwrecks, derailments and so on," said Andrew Stuart.

"It allows for everything," said Phileas Fogg. "It can be done."

"Then prove it!" challenged Andrew Stuart.

"Travel round the world in eighty days?" said Phileas Fogg.

"Yes."

"All right."

"When?"

"Straight away."

"This is ridiculous!" cried Andrew Stuart, beginning to get annoyed. "Let's get on with our game of whist." But a moment later, he put down his cards and said, "I'll bet four thousand pounds that it's impossible."

And Phileas Fogg took the bet. Indeed, he went further. He said he would bet *twenty thousand* pounds of his fortune that he would go round the world in eighty days. And his five card-playing friends accepted the bet.

"The Dover train leaves at 8.45 pm," he said. "I shall take it."

"This very evening?" asked Stuart.

"This very evening," replied Phileas Fogg. "Today is Wednesday, 2nd October. I must be back in this room by 8.45 pm on Saturday 21st December, or the twenty thousand pounds in my bank will belong to you, gentlemen."

The clock struck seven and the others suggested that they halted their card game so that Phileas Fogg could go home and prepare for his journey. But Mr Fogg assured them he was always prepared – and they played for another twenty-five minutes before he finally got up and left.

At 7.50 pm he opened the door of his house and walked in.

Passepartout was surprised. He had not expected to see Mr Fogg until after midnight. He had carefully examined the house in Savile Row and everything confirmed that his master was quiet and orderly, and not a man of surprises. This suited Passepartout. After many years of travels and adventure he was looking forward to leading a quiet life.

He was therefore astonished when his master announced that they would be leaving to catch the Dover train in ten minutes.

"Monsieur is going on a journey?" asked Passepartout.

"Yes," replied Phileas Fogg. "We're going round the world."

"Round the world?"

"In eighty days," said Phileas Fogg, calmly. "We will take a travelling bag with two woollen shirts and three pairs of socks. Everything else we can buy on the way."

By eight o'clock, the bewildered Passepartout had done as he had been asked. Mr Fogg took the travelling bag from him, put a thick wad of bank-notes into it, then gave it back.

"Take good care of it," he told Passepartout. "There's twenty thousand pounds inside."

They closed up the house and took a cab to Charing Cross Station. There, the five friends of Phileas Fogg had gathered to see him off, and he explained that he would have his passport stamped with a visa at every country he visited so that they would be able to see where he had been.

At 8.40 pm Phileas Fogg and his servant took their seats on the train. At 8.45 pm a whistle sounded and the train started moving. A fine rain was falling and both men were silent as the train travelled through the darkness. Then Passepartout let out a small cry of despair.

"I forgot to turn out the gas lamp in my bedroom!" he wailed.

"Well, young man," Mr Fogg replied coldly, "you will have to pay the bill when we get back!"

14

2

On Wednesday, 9th October, the steamer *Mongolia* was expected to arrive at Suez at eleven in the morning. Among the people waiting for it were two men. One was the British Consul at Suez, the other was a thin, impatient little man called Fix. He was one of the English detectives who had been sent to all the important ports after the Bank of England robbery. His job was to scrutinize all travellers passing through Suez and to follow anyone who looked suspicious, until the arrival of a warrant of arrest. Two days earlier, Mr Fix had received a description of the bank robber who was, apparently, a distinguished and well-dressed gentleman.

"How long will the steamer stay in Suez?" asked Fix.

"Four hours," said the Consul. "Long enough to take on sufficient coal for the thirteen hundred mile journey to Aden."

"And from Aden it goes straight on to Bombay?"

"Yes, without putting in anywhere."

Soon after, the *Mongolia* arrived. There were a good many passengers on board and some of them stayed on deck gazing out at the town. But most came ashore, and each one was watched carefully by Fix. Then one man asked Fix where he could find the British Consulate, and produced a passport which he apparently wished to have stamped with a British visa.

Fix took the passport and glanced rapidly at the description written inside it. It was exactly the same as the description of the robber which he had received from London! His hand shook with excitement.

"Is this yours?" he asked.

"No," the man replied, "it's my master's."

"Where is your master?" asked Fix.

"He has remained on board."

"He must go in person to the Consulate to establish his identity," said the inspector. He pointed to a house two hundred yards away. "The offices are at the corner of the square."

"Then I'll go and fetch my master, though he won't be pleased at having to come ashore." The passenger bowed and went back to the steamer.

The inspector hurried to the Consul's office to report.

"I've strong reasons for believing the robber is a passenger on the *Mongolia*," said Fix, and went on to tell the Consul how he had seen the man's servant and his passport.

"I doubt if the man will come to my office," said the Consul. "A thief doesn't like leaving traces of his journey behind him. Besides, passports are no longer compulsory."

"He'll come," said the inspector. "And his passport will be in order, to make us think he's an honest man. But I very much hope you won't visa it."

"If the passport is in order, I can't refuse," said the Consul.

"But I have to keep this man here until I can get a warrant for his arrest from London," said Fix.

15

"I can't help that," said the Consul.

At that moment there was a knock at the door and two men came in. One was Passepartout and the other was Phileas Fogg, who produced his passport and asked the Consul to be good enough to visa it.

The Consul read it carefully. "You are Mr Phileas Fogg?"

"Yes, sir," replied the gentleman.

"And this is your servant?"

"Yes, a Frenchman called Passepartout. We are going to Bombay."

"Very well, sir. You know that a visa is not necessary and that we no longer insist on seeing passports?" said the Consul.

"I know that," replied Mr Fogg. "But I want to be able to prove by your visa that I've been through Suez."

The passport was stamped and Mr Fogg paid the appropriate fee. Then he and Passepartout left.

"He looked perfectly honest," said the Consul.

"He also resembles in every detail the description of the robber," said Fix. "But I'm going to make sure."

Mr Fogg had gone back to the boat, but Passepartout was strolling along the quay. Fix quickly caught up with him.

"Well, my friend," said Fix. "Did you get your visa?"

"Oh, it's you, Monsieur," replied the Frenchman. "Yes, everything is in order." He looked dazed. "But we're travelling so fast I feel as if I'm in a dream. We were in Paris for only a little more than an hour!"

"You're in a hurry, are you?" said Fix.

"I'm not, but my master is. That reminds me, I must buy some socks and shirts. We left London with nothing but a small travelling bag."

"I'll take you to a bazaar where you'll find everything you want."

"That is very kind of you, Monsieur," said Passepartout.

They set off together, with Passepartout still talking.

"I must make sure I don't miss the boat," he said.

"You've plenty of time," replied Fix. "It's only twelve o'clock."

Passepartout took out his big watch. "Twelve o'clock? It's eight minutes to ten."

"Your watch is slow," said Fix. "You're still keeping London time, which is two hours earlier than Suez time. You must be careful to set your watch by the midday hour of each country."

"Me? Mess about with my watch? Never! It's a family heirloom," said Passepartout.

"Then it will never agree with the sun," said Fix.

"So much the worse for the sun, Monsieur! It's the sun that will be wrong!" And Passepartout put the watch back in his pocket.

A few moments later, Fix said, "So you left London in a hurry?"

"I should say we did! Last Wednesday, Mr Fogg came home from his club in the evening – which is quite unusual for him – and forty-five minutes later, we were off!"

"But where is your master going?" asked Fix.

"He's going round the world."

"Round the world?" exclaimed Fix.

16

"Yes, in eighty days! He says it's a bet, but I don't believe it," said Passepartout. "There must be another reason."

"So Mr Fogg is a bit of an eccentric," said Fix. "Is he rich?"

"He must be, and he's brought a lot of money with him, in brand new banknotes. And he's not mean, because he's promised the *Mongolia*'s chief engineer a splendid bonus if we get to Bombay well ahead of time."

"Have you known your master for a long time?"

"I only became his servant the day we set off," said Passepartout.

It is easy to imagine how excited Fix became at these replies. The hasty departure from London shortly after the robbery; the large sum of money which Fogg had brought with him; this urge to get to a distant country quickly, supposedly because of an eccentric bet. All this convinced Fix that he was right.

"Is it a long way to Bombay?" asked Passepartout.

"Another ten days sailing," said Fix.

He left Passepartout at the bazaar and hurried back to the Consul.

"I've got my man," he said. "He's pretending to be an eccentric who's trying to travel around the world in eighty days."

"But why did he ask for a visa to prove that he had been through Suez?" asked the Consul.

"I've no idea, sir," replied Fix, "but listen to this." And in a few words, he repeated his conversation with Fogg's servant.

"Send a telegram to London asking for a warrant for his arrest to be sent to me in Bombay. Then I shall go to India aboard the *Mongolia* and, once on British soil again, I shall put my hand on Mr Fogg's shoulder and present him with the warrant."

With that, the inspector rushed off to the telegraph office.

3

DURING THE VOYAGE to Bombay, Phileas Fogg rarely came on deck to observe the passing scenery. He spent most of his time playing whist with some other card enthusiasts who were making the trip. This gave Fix an opportunity to become friendly with Passepartout – something the inspector decided might prove useful for the future. He often bought Passepartout a drink in the bar, and soon learned that the weary servant was hoping Mr Fogg would bring his round-the-world journey to an end in Bombay.

The *Mongolia* arrived on the 20th October, two days earlier than expected. At half-past four in the afternoon, the steamer came alongside the quay, and the passengers went ashore. The train for Calcutta was due to leave at eight o'clock, and Phileas Fogg sent Passepartout to do some shopping whilst he took himself off to the passport office.

Meanwhile, Mr Fix hurried to the headquarters of the Bombay police. Had they received a warrant from London? They had not. Fix was extremely annoyed. He tried to persuade the Chief of Police to give him a warrant for Fogg's arrest, but the Chief refused. This was a matter for the London police, he told Fix. So the inspector could only wait. However, he was sure Phileas Fogg would stay in Bombay for a while, and this would give the warrant time to arrive.

Passepartout had realised that his journey was not, as he had hoped, at an end. He now knew that his master would go on at least as far as Calcutta, and perhaps even further. He began to wonder whether this bet of Mr Fogg's might not be perfectly serious after all.

He bought some shirts and socks, then wandered through the streets of Bombay. Passepartout was fascinated by all that he saw, but he was on his way to the railway station when he passed in front of the beautiful temple on Malabar Hill. He immediately became curious and wanted to look inside.

Unfortunately, there were two things Passepartout did not know. One was that Christians were strictly forbidden to enter Hindu temples. The other was that even the Hindus themselves would not enter without first removing their shoes and leaving them outside.

Passepartout went innocently into the temple like any tourist – and was knocked to the floor by three priests! They tore off his shoes and socks, and began hitting him hard.

The Frenchman was both strong and agile. He sprang to his feet and, with a punch and a kick, knocked down the three priests and ran from the building-ing as fast as he could.

At five to eight, only a few minutes before the Calcutta train was due to leave, Passepartout arrived at the station hatless, barefoot, and without his shopping which he had lost in the scuffle.

Fix was on the platform, having followed Mr Fogg to the station and realised that the scoundrel was going to leave Bombay. He had made up his mind to follow Fogg to Calcutta, and further, if necessary. Passepartout did not see Fix, who was standing in the shadows, but Fix overheard Passepartout telling his master about his adventures. What Fix heard made him change his mind.

"I'll stay here," he said, smiling to himself. "An offence committed on Indian soil ... I've got my man!"

Just then, the train gave a loud whistle and moved out of the station.

Passepartout travelled in the same compartment as his master, and in the opposite corner sat another man. He was tall, with fair hair, and his name was Sir Francis Cromarty. He was a brigadier in the Indian Army and had been one of Mr Fogg's whist partners during the voyage from Suez. He also knew a great deal about the history and customs of India.

Sir Francis thought Phileas Fogg to be one of the strangest men he had ever met, and when he heard the reason for Mr Fogg's journey around the world, he considered it to be nothing less than eccentric, and serving no useful purpose. From time to time, Sir Francis and Phileas Fogg exchanged a few words. The brigadier told his travelling companion that there had been a risk of trouble after Passepartout's adventure in the temple.

"The British Government is very strict about that sort of offence," said Sir Francis. "It insists on respect for the religious customs of the Hindus, and if your servant had been caught ..."

"He would have been convicted, served his sentence, then gone quietly back to Europe," said Mr Fogg. "I don't see how that matter could have delayed me."

The next day, the train stopped briefly at Burhanpur, and Passepartout was able to buy a pair of Indian slippers which were decorated with false pearls. Until his arrival in Bombay, Passepartout had believed that things would go no further, but now that they were travelling at full speed across India, he had changed his outlook. Now he took his master's plans seriously and began to worry about possible delays, and accidents which might happen on the way. He felt very bad about his stupidity at the temple. He could easily have been the cause of his master losing the bet.

The following day was the 22nd October. In reply to a question from Sir Francis Cromarty, Passepartout looked at his watch and said it was three in the morning. Sir Francis corrected him, saying that it was at least seven and that Passepartout's watch was four hours slow. He tried to make him understand that as they were going eastwards, towards the sun, each day became shorter by four minutes for every degree they covered. It was all in vain. Passepartout refused to alter his precious watch.

At eight in the morning the train came to a stop in what seemed the middle of nowhere, and the guard walked along it shouting, "All change!"

Passepartout jumped down on to the track to see what was happening and came back almost at once. "Monsieur, there's no more railway!" he said.

"What do you mean?" asked Sir Francis.

"I mean the train doesn't go any farther!"

Sir Francis got out at once, and Phileas Fogg followed him without hurrying.

"Where are we?" Sir Francis asked the guard.

"At the village of Kholby," the guard replied.

"Do we stop here?"

"Of course. The railway isn't finished."

"What! It isn't finished?"

"No," said the guard. "There are still fifty miles of track to be laid from here to Allahabad, where the line starts again."

"But the papers said that the whole line was open."

"Well, the papers were wrong, sir."

"But you issue tickets from Bombay to Calcutta!" said Sir Francis, who was beginning to get angry.

"That's true," replied the guard. "But the passengers know that they have to find their own means of transport from Kholby to Allahabad."

Sir Francis Cromarty was furious, and Passepartout wanted to knock down the guard. He did not dare look at his master.

"Sir Francis," said Phileas Fogg, calmly. "If you are agreeable, we will see about finding a way of getting to Allahabad."

"But Mr Fogg, isn't this delay bound to upset your plans?"

22 "No, Sir Francis, I was prepared for it."

"What! You mean that you knew the line – ?"

"No, but I knew some obstacle or other would crop up sooner or later. There is no harm done. I have two days in hand. A steamer leaves Calcutta for Hong Kong on the 25th, and today is only the 22nd. We shall get to Calcutta in time."

Most of the travellers had known about the unfinished line and had been quick to seize all the carts and carriages, horses and oxen which the village could provide. By the time Sir Francis and Mr Fogg went to look, everything had been taken.

"I shall walk," said Phileas Fogg.

But Passepartout had been more fortunate in his search. "Monsieur, I think I have found a means of transport," he said.

"What is it?" asked Mr Fogg.

"An elephant. It belongs to an Indian who lives nearby."

The elephant was a half-tamed animal, but Mr Fogg offered the owner the considerable sum of ten pounds an hour for the hire of the beast. This was refused. Twenty pounds? No. Forty? No. Then Phileas Fogg suggested buying the animal, and he offered the owner one thousand pounds. Once again, the owner refused.

Sir Francis took Mr Fogg to one side and urged him to think again before offering any more. Phileas Fogg reminded the brigadier that a bet of twenty thousand pounds was at stake and that he simply had to have the elephant. He then went back to the owner and offered twelve hundred pounds, then fifteen hundred, then eighteen hundred, and at last two thousand pounds. The Indian accepted. Mr Fogg had his elephant.

He paid with banknotes from the travelling bag. Then a young Parsee with an intelligent face offered his services as a guide and was given the job. The young man fixed a seat on each side of the elephant's back and, after buying food from the village, Sir Francis and Mr Fogg each took a seat on the elephant whilst Passepartout sat between them, astride the animal's back. The Parsee perched himself on the elephant's neck.

At nine o'clock, they left the village and headed for the dense forest of palm trees around it.

4

THE PARSEE, who was familiar with the roads and paths of the region, claimed he could save twenty miles by cutting across the forest, and they took his word for it. By eight in the evening, after travelling all day and with just a brief stop for lunch, they had crossed the Vindhai Mountains and had stopped for the night.

At six in the morning, they set off again, descending the last of the mountain slopes. The guide hoped to reach Allahabad that evening, but at four o'clock in the afternoon the elephant suddenly stopped in its tracks.

"What's the matter?" asked Sir Francis.

"I don't know, sir," replied the Parsee.

Moments later, they heard the sound of many voices and loud music.

The anxious guide jumped down, tied the elephant to a tree and plunged into the thickest part of the wood. He returned after a few minutes.

"A Hindu procession is coming this way," he told the others. "We must keep out of sight if we can."

They hid in the trees and watched the procession pass by. First came some priests. These were surrounded by men, women and children chanting some sort of funeral song, interrupted at regular intervals by tom-tom drums and cymbals. Behind them came a carriage carrying a hideous statue. The statue had four arms, a dark red body, and ghastly staring eyes.

"The goddess of Kali," murmured Sir Francis. "The goddess of love and death."

"Of death perhaps, but of love never!" said Passepartout.

Behind this were some priests in long robes, and they were dragging along a woman who was hardly able to stand. She was young, very beautiful, and wore a gold-spangled tunic covered with a thin veil.

Guards walked behind her with sabres and pistols at their belts. They were carrying the dead body of an old man. The corpse was dressed in the magnificent clothes of a rajah.

More musicians completed the procession.

"A suttee," said Sir Francis.

The Parsee nodded as the procession disappeared into the forest.

"What's a suttee?" asked Phileas Fogg.

"A human sacrifice," explained the brigadier. "That woman you have just
seen will be burnt at dawn tomorrow."

"Oh, the scoundrels!" cried Passepartout.

"And the corpse?" asked Mr Fogg.

"That is the body of her husband, a prince," said the Parsee.

"In most of India," said Sir Francis, "these sacrifices have been stopped, but we can do nothing in the wilder regions."

"Poor woman!" said Passepartout. "To be burnt alive!"

"Yes, but if she were not you can't imagine what cruelties she would have to suffer. Her relatives would shave off her hair, feed her on a few handfuls of rice, and leave her to die in a corner like some mangy dog. Many women prefer to die rather than face that."

The guide was shaking his head. "That woman doesn't want to die, she is being forced. Everyone in the area knows her story. Her name is Aouda and she was made to marry that old prince. Three months later, he died and, knowing the fate which awaited her, Aouda escaped. But she was recaptured almost immediately. The prince's family will get the old man's fortune if that girl dies, and have arranged for her to be sacrificed."

"But she seemed to be offering no resistance," said Sir Francis.

"That's because she'd been drugged," replied the Parsee.

"Where are they taking her?" asked Phileas Fogg.

"To the temple at Pillagi, two miles from here. She will spend the night there, waiting for the hour of her death."

"And when will that be?"

"Tomorrow, at the first sign of day."

Just as they were about to move on, Phileas Fogg said, "What if we were to rescue this woman?"

"Rescue the woman, Mr Fogg!" cried the brigadier.

"I've got twelve hours to spare, I can use them for that."

The plan was a daring one, bristling with difficulties. Mr Fogg was going to risk his life, and therefore the success of his journey, but he did not hesitate. Fortunately, the others were only too happy to help him save this poor woman if they could.

Half an hour later, they came to a copse five hundred yards from the temple where the young woman was a prisoner. Methods of reaching her were discussed, but it was decided that whatever they did would have to be done at night and not in the morning when the victim was taken out to die.

They waited until six o'clock, when it was dark, then went closer to the temple to see what could be done. Everything was quiet. Sleeping figures, overcome by heavy drinking, lay on the ground in the clearing. Behind them, between the trees, loomed the temple of Pillagi. But to the guide's great disappointment, guards were pacing up and down outside the temple with their swords drawn. And it was reasonable to assume that the priests inside were also awake and keeping watch.

"Let's wait," said the brigadier. "It's still early, and perhaps the guards will fall asleep too."

They waited until midnight, but there was no change in the situation. It was clear the guards did not mean to sleep, so they decided to enter the temple by making a hole in the wall. But would the priests inside also be on the alert?

The night was dark, the moon shrouded with thick clouds, and they managed to get down to the back of the temple without being seen. There were no guards on this side, but then there were no doors or windows to watch. Phileas Fogg and his companions had only pocket knives to work with but fortunately the walls were made of bricks and wood, and once the first brick had been removed the others would come away easily.

They went to work, making as little noise as possible, but after a few minutes a cry came from inside the temple and other cries answered it from outside. Quickly, they retreated to the trees again, and soon after some guards appeared and took up positions at the rear of the temple. After that there seemed nothing more that Mr Fogg and his friends could do.

"We'll wait," said Phileas Fogg. "I need not be in Allahabad before noon tomorrow."

"But what can you hope to do?" asked Sir Francis. "It will soon be daylight and —"

"And perhaps the chance we are hoping for will come at the last moment," said Mr Fogg.

The guide led them to a safer place at the front of the clearing. There, 28 sheltered by a clump of trees, they could watch the sleeping groups.

Passepartout was perched on the lowest branch of a tree. An idea came to him and he started to make a plan. Soon after, he began to crawl along the branch, the end of which hung down towards the ground.

The hours passed until there were a few lighter patches in the sky, though it was still very dark. The slumbering crowd began to wake up. Chants and cries broke out. The time had come for the poor woman to die.

The temple doors opened and Phileas Fogg and Sir Francis Cromarty could see the victim being dragged outside by two priests. The crowd moved forward towards the pile of wood – the funeral pyre – where the sacrifice would take place. The body of the dead prince was already on top of it. The crowd stopped fifty yards from the funeral pyre and, in the semi-darkness, Phileas Fogg and his companions saw the young woman, still under the influence of the drugs, stretched out beside her dead husband.

The wood had been soaked with oil and it flared up immediately it was set alight. Sir Francis and the guide held back Phileas Fogg who tried to dash towards the pyre in a noble if foolish attempt to save the girl.

Suddenly, a cry of terror arose and the whole crowd fell to the ground in horror. The old prince was not dead! He was rising up like a ghost, picking up the young woman in his arms and coming down through the smoke and flames of the pyre! Seized with terror, the priests and others lay with their faces to the ground, too afraid to look up.

Mr Fogg, Sir Francis and the guide watched as the figure approached them, carrying the girl. They, too, were astounded. Then the figure spoke. "Let's clear off!"

It was Passepartout!

Under cover of darkness he had secretly gone to the funeral pyre, put on some of the dead prince's clothes and, lying down beside the corpse, had waited until the moment the fire had been lit. He had then snatched the young woman from the jaws of death and walked through the terrified crowd.

Moments later, they had disappeared into the wood and the elephant was carrying them off at a brisk trot. The young woman, still asleep, was wrapped in travelling rugs. But the sound of shouts, cries, and even a bullet which made a hole in Phileas Fogg's hat, told them that their trick had been discovered. The old prince's body was now clearly visible amongst the flames and the priests, realising they had been fooled, had rushed into the forest with the guards. But they were too late.

The elephant moved quickly through the trees, and an hour later Passepartout was still chuckling over his triumph. At seven o'clock the party halted and the guide made the young woman swallow a few mouthfuls of brandy and water. Sir Francis was worried about her future. He told Phileas Fogg that if she remained in India she would certainly be caught again by the people who wanted to kill her. Phileas Fogg replied that he would bear these remarks in mind and take the necessary steps.

At ten o'clock, they arrived at Allahabad, where the railway began again. From there, it was only twenty-four hours to Calcutta so Phileas Fogg would get there in time to catch the steamer leaving for Hong Kong at noon on the 25th October.

5

THE YOUNG WOMAN was left in a waiting room at the station, and Passepartout was sent to buy the clothes and other things she would need. By the time he returned, Aouda was beginning to recover consciousness.

The train was now about to leave Allahabad but there was still the question of what to do with the elephant. But Phileas Fogg had already made up his mind.

"Parsee," he said to the guide, "you have given me good and faithful service. Would you like this elephant?"

The guide's eyes shone. "Your honour is giving me a fortune!"

"Take it, my friend," said Phileas Fogg. "It is yours."

A few minutes later, Phileas Fogg, Sir Francis Cromarty and Passepartout were sitting in a comfortable railway carriage with Aouda. During the journey, the young woman regained consciousness completely and was astonished to find herself on a train, dressed in European clothes, and in the company of complete strangers!

The brigadier told her what had happened, making special mention of Mr Fogg's kindness and of Passepartout's bold rescue. Aouda thanked them, more with her tears than her words, but she was still afraid of what was to happen to her. To put her mind at rest, but speaking in a cool manner, Phileas Fogg offered to take her to Hong Kong. Aouda accepted gratefully. As it happened, she said, she had a relative living in Hong Kong who was one of the leading merchants in that city.

At half-past twelve, the train came to Benares, which was where Sir Francis Cromarty would have to leave them to rejoin his troops. He said farewell and wished Phileas Fogg every success with the journey around the world. Then they parted.

They arrived in Calcutta at seven in the morning. The steamer was not due to leave until noon, so Phileas Fogg had five hours to spare. But just as he was about to leave the station, a policeman came up to him.

"Mr Phileas Fogg?"

"That is my name."

"Is this man your servant?" asked the policeman, pointing at Passepartout.

"Yes."

"Will both of you kindly come along with me."

Mr Fogg showed no sign of surprise. Passepartout tried to argue but Phileas Fogg told him to obey.

"May this young lady come with us?" asked Mr Fogg.

"She may," replied the policeman.

The policeman took them to a four-wheeled carriage with two horses, and they got in. Nobody spoke during the twenty minute journey.

At the police station, they were taken to a room with barred windows. They were told that they would be brought before a judge at half-past eight, then the policeman went out and shut the door.

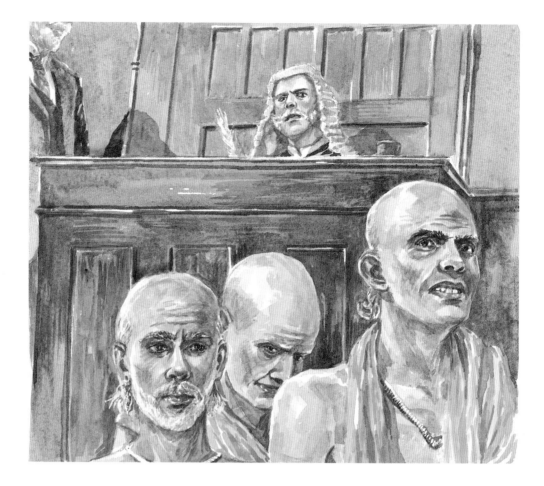

Aouda spoke quickly to Phileas Fogg. "Sir, you must leave me! It is because you rescued me that you are to be prosecuted."

Phileas Fogg merely replied that he could not believe it. Who would come forward to make the charge? Not the priests or relatives of the old prince. They would not dare to go to the law for help in such a thing as a human sacrifice. No, there was some mistake. In any case, Mr Fogg said, he would not abandon the young woman but would take her to Hong Kong.

"But the boat leaves at noon!" said Passepartout.

"And we shall be on it," replied the unflappable Phileas Fogg.

At eight-thirty, they were taken before the judge.

"The first case," said the judge.

"Phileas Fogg?" said the clerk.

"Here," replied Mr Fogg.

"Passepartout?"

"Present!" replied Passepartout.

"Good!" said the judge. "Prisoners at the bar, for two days the police have been looking for you on every train from Bombay."

"But what are we accused of?" cried Passepartout, losing patience.

"You will soon find out," answered the judge.

Then, at an order from him, the door opened and three Hindu priests were brought in.

"Just as I thought," muttered Passepartout. "Those are the scoundrels who
34 were trying to burn our young lady!"

The priests stood in front of the judge, and the clerk of the court read out the charge against Passepartout and Phileas Fogg. They were accused of sacrilege; of violating a holy temple.

"You have heard the charge?" the judge asked Phileas Fogg.

"Yes sir," replied Mr Fogg, looking at his watch. "And I admit it."

"Ah! You admit it?"

"Yes, and I'm waiting for these three priests to admit what they were going to do at the Pillagi temple."

The three priests looked at one another. They did not seem to understand what Mr Fogg was saying.

"Why, yes!" burst out Passepartout. "At the Pillagi temple where they were going to burn their victim!"

"Burn whom?" said the judge, completely bewildered. "In the heart of Bombay?"

"Bombay?" exclaimed Passepartout.

"Yes, Bombay. This has nothing to do with the temple of Pillagi, but with the temple at Malabar Hill in Bombay."

"And as proof," added the clerk, "here are the shoes." And he placed a pair of shoes on his desk.

"My shoes!" cried Passepartout.

Phileas Fogg and his servant had completely forgotten the incident in the Bombay temple. But Fix, the detective, had not. He had stayed in Bombay and persuaded the three priests to go to court, promising them heavy damages. He knew that the British government treated very severely the kind of offence Passepartout had committed. Then Fix and the priests had travelled to Calcutta by the next train, carrying a warrant for Passepartout's arrest.

Because of the time taken to rescue Aouda, Fix and the priests had arrived in Calcutta first. Fix had been puzzled by Mr Fogg's delay and was worried that his man had got off at another station and had taken refuge in the northern provinces. It was a great relief to the detective when he saw Mr Fogg get off the train that morning, even if the gentleman did have a young lady with him whose identity Fix did not know.

Now, in the court-room, Passepartout had not noticed Fix sitting in the corner. He was too busy listening to the judge.

"You admit the shoes are yours?" asked the judge.

"The fact is admitted," replied Mr Fogg, coldly.

"According to English law," said the judge, "the religions of the people of India have strict protection and, as the defendant Passepartout has admitted his crime, I hereby sentence him to fourteen days in prison and a fine of three hundred pounds.

"Three hundred pounds?" exclaimed Passepartout.

"Silence!" shouted the clerk.

"And," added the judge, "because we can't be sure Mr Fogg had nothing to do with the matter, and because he is responsible for the actions of his servant, I hereby sentence Phileas Fogg to seven days in prison and a fine of one hundred and fifty pounds. Clerk, call the next case!"

Fix, watching from his corner of the room, was delighted. The warrant from London was sure to come within the next seven days.

Passepartout was dumbfounded. The sentence would ruin his master. The twenty thousand pound bet would be lost, and all because, like a fool, he had gone into that temple.

But Phileas Fogg remained quite calm. "I wish to offer bail," he said.

"You are entitled to do so," replied the judge.

Fix felt a shiver run down his spine, but recovered when he heard the judge fix bail at the enormous sum of one thousand pounds each.

"Here is the money," said Phileas Fogg.

And from the bag Passepartout was carrying he took a wad of banknotes which he placed on the clerk's desk.

"This money will be returned to you when you leave prison," said the judge. "In the meantime, you are released on bail."

"Come along," Phileas Fogg said to his servant.

"They might at least return my shoes," said Passepartout, angrily.

His shoes were given back to him.

"They have cost over a thousand pounds each!" he muttered. "And they aren't even comfortable!"

An unhappy Passepartout followed Mr Fogg and Aouda out of the court-room. Fix was still hoping Phileas Fogg would decide against parting with the

two thousand pounds and serve his seven day sentence in prison. The detective hurried after Mr Fogg to see what the strange man was going to do next.

Mr Fogg took a carriage and he, Aouda and Passepartout climbed into it. Fix ran behind until the carriage reached the quayside. There, half a mile out at sea, the *Rangoon* lay at anchor.

Eleven o'clock was striking. Mr Fogg was one hour early.

Fix saw Mr Fogg get out of the carriage and into a small boat with Aouda and his servant. The detective stamped his foot.

"The scoundrel is leaving!" he exclaimed. "Two thousand pounds thrown away! He's a spendthrift as well as a thief! Oh! I'll follow him to the ends of the earth if need be, but if he goes on at this rate there'll be nothing left of the stolen money!"

The police inspector had a good reason for making this remark. For in fact, since leaving London, what with fares, bribes, the purchase of an elephant, fines and bail, Phileas Fogg had already thrown away more than five thousand pounds. And the detective's reward – a percentage of the money that was finally recovered – was steadily getting smaller.

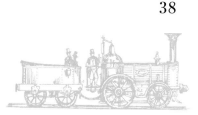

6

THE *RANGOON* would take only eleven or twelve days to do the 3500 mile journey, and during the first few days of the voyage Aouda came to know Phileas Fogg much better. She took every opportunity to thank him for all he had done, but Mr Fogg listened to her in what seemed a very cool manner, showing no emotion at all. He made certain that she had everything she wanted, saw her regularly at certain hours, and was always extremely polite. But Aouda did not know what to think of him. Passepartout explained about his master's eccentric character and told her about the bet which was the cause of their journey around the world. Aouda spoke about her family, and in particular about the wealthy uncle whom she hoped to join in Hong Kong.

But what of Inspector Fix? He had left instructions at Calcutta for the warrant from London to be sent on to him at Hong Kong, whenever it finally arrived. He then managed to get aboard the *Rangoon* without being seen by Passepartout, and hoped to keep his presence a secret until the steamer arrived at its destination.

All the inspector's hopes were pinned on Hong Kong. The arrest must be made there or the robber would escape him, for Hong Kong was the last British soil they would meet with on the journey. Beyond lay China, Japan and America, where Fogg would be safe from the English warrant. In those countries, Fix would need an extradition order, which would mean delays and difficulties, all of which would enable Fogg to escape once and for all. No, the arrest had to be made at Hong Kong.

The inspector was also puzzled by the presence of Aouda. Who was this woman? How had she become Fogg's companion? Had they met by chance, or had Fogg come to India to meet her? Perhaps she was on the *Rangoon* against her will! Perhaps Fogg had kidnapped her! If this was the case, Fix could create such difficulties at Hong Kong that no amount of money would save Fogg from prison.

Eventually, the detective decided to question Passepartout and, the day before the *Rangoon* reached Singapore, Passepartout suddenly found himself face to face with Fix.

"Monsieur Fix!" cried Passepartout. "Well I never! I leave you in Bombay, and find you on the way to Hong Kong! Are you going round the world too?"

"No, no," answered Fix. "I intend to stop at Hong Kong, for a few days at least."

"But how is it I haven't seen you on board since we left Calcutta?"

"I haven't been too well – a bit of sea-sickness – and I've been in my cabin," said Fix. "But how is your master, Mr Phileas Fogg?"

"In the best of health and not a day behind schedule!" replied Passepartout. "And now we have a young lady with us."

"A young lady?" said the detective, pretending to be surprised.

Passepartout told him the whole story – the incident in the Bombay temple, the purchase of the elephant for two thousand pounds, the episode of the 39 suttee, the rescue of Aouda, the sentence of the court and the release of Phileas Fogg's party on bail. Fix, who knew the last part of the story, pretended to know nothing at all, and Passepartout was pleased to have a listener who showed so much interest.

"But does your master intend to take this lady with him to Europe?" asked Fix.

"Oh no, Monsieur Fix. We are placing her in the care of an uncle of hers in Hong Kong," said Passepartout.

The detective hid his disappointment. Any chance of making fresh trouble for Phileas Fogg had faded away.

After this, Passepartout and the detective often met, but Fix made no attempt to get the servant to talk. As for Passepartout, he began to think seriously about the strange chance which had once again placed Fix on the same route as his master. The coincidence was striking, to put it mildly. What was this fellow up to? Passepartout was ready to bet his slippers that Fix would leave Hong Kong at the same time as they did, and probably on the same steamer.

Not in a hundred years would Passepartout have guessed the real reason Fix was following them. He would never have imagined that Phileas Fogg was being shadowed round the world like a thief. Instead, he found another explanation. Fix, Passepartout decided, had been sent by the members of the Reform Club, to make sure the journey was properly carried out along the agreed route.

'It's obvious!' thought Passepartout. 'He's a spy those gentlemen have hired to trail us! What a low thing to do!' And he decided to say nothing to his master for fear of upsetting him.

At four o'clock on the morning of Thursday, 31st October, the *Rangoon* put in to Singapore to refuel, having gained half a day on its schedule. Phileas Fogg went ashore with Aouda, who wanted to go driving for a few hours. A suspicious Fix followed them without letting himself be seen, and Passepartout, who was amused by the detective's antics, went off to do his usual shopping.

After a two hour drive in a pretty carriage drawn by two horses, Phileas Fogg and Aouda returned to the steamer, unaware that they had been followed by Fix, who had been forced to hire a carriage like theirs.

At eleven o'clock the *Rangoon*, having taken on coal, steamed out of Singapore. Thirteen hundred miles separated Singapore from Hong Kong, a small English colony off the coast of China. It was important for Phileas Fogg to cover this distance in six days at the most if he was to catch the boat due to leave Hong Kong on 6th November. It would take him to Yokohama, one of the chief ports of Japan.

The weather, which had been fine until then, suddenly changed. The sea became very rough, and there was a moderate gale blowing from the south-east. Luckily, this was the right direction for the steamer, and the captain often raised the sails to assist the speed of the vessel.

Nevertheless, time was lost because of the bad weather and this infuriated Passepartout who blamed the captain, the chief engineer and the steamer company. Mr Fogg, on the other hand, remained quite calm.

"Are you really in such a hurry to get to Hong Kong?" Fix asked Passepartout one day.

"A tremendous hurry!" replied Passepartout.

"You think Mr Fogg is anxious to catch the boat to Yokohama."

"Frightfully anxious."

"So now you believe in this peculiar journey around the world?"

"Absolutely. What about you, Monsieur Fix?"

"Me? I don't believe a word of it!"

"You're a sly one!" replied Passepartout with a wink.

This remark made the inspector think. Had the Frenchman found out that he was a detective? No, how could he? But the man clearly knew something, or thought he did. Fix made a decision. If he could not arrest Fogg in Hong Kong, then he would tell Passepartout everything. Either the servant was his master's partner in crime, or he knew nothing about the robbery. And if he knew nothing, it would be in Passepartout's interest to help Fix make the arrest, otherwise the servant could find himself in serious trouble.

During the last few days of the voyage, the weather was rather rough. On the 3rd and 4th November there was a gale and all sails had to be taken in. The steamer's speed slowed considerably and it was estimated that they would reach Hong Kong twenty hours behind time, and even more if the storm did not die down. This delay would be enough to make Phileas Fogg miss the boat to Yokohama, but he seemed quite undismayed by this prospect.

The storm delighted Fix, even if it did make him sea-sick. It was a small price to pay for a delay which would keep Mr Fogg in Hong Kong for a few extra days.

But Passepartout found it difficult to conceal his anger. He was exasperated by the storm and remained on deck throughout it. A hundred times he questioned the captain, officers and sailors, insisting on knowing how long the storm would last, but they just laughed and pointed to the barometer which showed no signs of rising.

At last the storm died down and the sea grew calmer. Once more the sails were hoisted up and the *Rangoon* forged ahead at full speed.

However, it was impossible to make up for lost time and it was five o'clock in the morning of the 6th November that land was at last sighted. The *Rangoon* was twenty-four hours late, and Phileas Fogg had missed the steamer to Yokohama.

At six o'clock the pilot came on board the *Rangoon* and took his place on the bridge to guide the ship into Hong Kong harbour. Mr Fogg asked him if he knew when there would be a boat leaving Hong Kong for Yokohama.

"Tomorrow, on the morning tide," replied the pilot.

"Ah!" said Mr Fogg, without showing the slightest surprise.

Passepartout, who was with them, wanted to hug the pilot, while Fix would gladly have wrung the pilot's neck.

"What's the ship's name?" asked Mr Fogg.

"The *Carnatic*," the pilot replied.

"Wasn't the *Carnatic* due to sail yesterday?"

43

"Yes, sir, but they had to repair one of its boilers, so her sailing was put off until tomorrow."

"Thank you," said Mr Fogg.

By one o'clock the passengers were going ashore. Phileas Fogg had been very lucky. If one of the *Carnatic*'s boilers had not needed repairing, the steamer would have left on the 5th November, and the travellers bound for Japan would have had to wait a week for the next ship. True, Mr Fogg was twenty-four hours behind, but this delay was not too serious, for the ship which sailed from Yokohama to San Francisco always waited for the steamer from Hong Kong to arrive. And the twenty-four hours lost could easily be made up during the voyage across the Pacific.

As the *Carnatic* was not due to sail until five o'clock the next morning, Mr Fogg had sixteen hours in Hong Kong. He took rooms at the Club Hotel, then left Aouda and Passepartout there whilst he drove to the Stock Exchange. He was sure that Aouda's uncle – a rich merchant – would be well known there, and indeed he was. However, as one of the stockbrokers explained, Aouda's uncle had made his fortune and had gone to live in Europe – in Holland, it was thought.

Phileas Fogg returned to the Club Hotel and immediately went to see Aouda. He told her the news of her uncle.

"What must I do, Mr Fogg?" she asked, after she had listened to him.

"It is very simple," he replied. "Return with us to Europe."

"But I can't cause you so much trouble – "

"It's no trouble. Your presence will not interfere in any way with my programme. Passepartout, go to the *Carnatic* and book three cabins."

Delighted to think that he would not be losing the company of this charming young lady, Passepartout promptly left the hotel.

7

PASSEPARTOUT made his way to the harbour and to the quay from which the *Carnatic* was due to sail. He was not at all surprised to see Fix there, walking up and down with a disappointed look on his face.

The detective had good reason for looking as he did, for the warrant from London had not yet arrived and it seemed that Phileas Fogg was going to escape yet again.

"Mr Fix!" said Passepartout, smiling. "Have you decided to come with us as far as America?"

"Yes," replied Fix between clenched teeth.

Passepartout laughed loudly. "I knew you couldn't bear to leave us!"

The two men went into the shipping office to book their cabins. The clerk told them that as the *Carnatic's* repairs had been completed, the steamer would leave that very evening at eight o'clock and not the following morning, as announced.

"Splendid!" said Passepartout. "I'll go and tell my master."

At that moment, Fix made a decision. He decided to tell Passepartout everything, for it seemed this was his only chance of detaining Phileas Fogg in Hong Kong for a few days.

After they came out of the shipping office, Fix offered to buy his companion a drink. They went into a tavern on the quay and found themselves in a large, well-decorated room where about thirty people sat at small tables, drinking. At the far end of the room was a bed covered with cushions, and on this bed lay a number of sleeping figures.

Fix and Passepartout realised that they had entered a place where opium was smoked, one of many such places in Hong Kong. They ordered two bottles of port, and the Frenchman began to drink steadily as Fix watched him. They chatted about this and that, until Passepartout remembered that he had to go and tell his master that the sailing time for the *Carnatic* had been changed. He got up to go.

Fix held him back. "Just a moment. I want to talk to you about a serious matter."

"A serious matter?" exclaimed Passepartout, gulping down the last few drops of port from the bottom of his glass. "Talk to me about it tomorrow, I haven't time today."

"Wait," said Fix. "It's to do with your master."

Something in the expression on Fix's face made Passepartout sit down again. "What have you got to tell me?" he asked.

Fix put a hand on his companion's arm and lowered his voice. "You've guessed who I am, haven't you?"

"Of course I have!" said Passepartout with a smile.

"Then I'm going to tell you everything."

"First let me tell you that those gentlemen of yours are wasting their money," said Passepartout.

"It's easy for you to talk," said Fix. "It's clear you don't know how much is involved."

"Twenty thousand pounds!" replied Passepartout.

"*Fifty-five* thousand pounds!" said Fix.

"What!" cried Passepartout. "Fifty-five thousand pounds! Well, that's all the more reason for not wasting a moment." He stood up again.

"Fifty-five thousand pounds," Fix went on, ordering a bottle of brandy and making Passepartout sit down again. "And if I'm successful, I get a reward of two thousand pounds. Would you like five hundred of it for helping me?"

"Helping you?" exclaimed Passepartout, his eyes like saucers.

"Yes, helping me to keep Mr Fogg in Hong Kong for a few days."

"What!" cried Passepartout. "Not only do those gentlemen want my master followed, they want to put obstacles in his way! Shame on them!"

"What do you mean?" asked Fix, bewildered.

"I mean it's a dirty trick. They might just as well take the money out of Mr Fogg's pocket!"

"That's just what we hope to do in the end," said Fix.

"And they call themselves friends!" exclaimed Passepartout. "Members of the Reform Club! My master is an honest man, Mr Fix, and when he makes a bet he expects to win it fairly."

Fix stared hard at Passepartout. "Wait a minute, just who do you think I am?"

"Why, a spy hired by the members of the Reform Club to check my master's route. I guessed who you were some time ago, but I've been careful not to tell Mr Fogg."

"He knows nothing?" Fix asked eagerly.

"Not a thing," replied Passepartout, draining his glass again.

The police inspector hesitated. What should he do? Passepartout's mistake seemed genuine. It was also clear that the servant had nothing to do with the robbery. Once again, the detective made a decision.

"Listen carefully," he said. "I'm not what you think I am. I haven't been sent by the members of the Reform Club."

Passepartout grinned. "I don't believe you."

"I'm a police inspector from London," Fix went on, "and I can prove it. Here is my warrant card."

He took the card from his wallet and showed the other man. Passepartout stared at it, unable to utter a word.

"Mr Fogg's bet is just a trick," said Fix. "He's fooled you *and* the members of the Reform Club."

"But why?" said Passepartout.

"Listen. On 29th September, fifty-five thousand pounds was stolen from the Bank of England. We have a description of the thief, and that description fits Mr Fogg exactly."

"Nonsense!" exclaimed Passepartout, striking the table with his fist. "My master is the most honest man in the world!"

"How do you know?" said Fix. "You don't even know him. You became his servant on the very day of his departure, and he left in a great hurry giving a ridiculous reason, without any luggage, and taking with him a huge sum in banknotes! And you're telling me he's an honest man!"

"Yes, yes!" said Passepartout.

"Do you want to be arrested as his accomplice?"

Passepartout put his head in his hands. He did not want to believe his master was a bank robber, yet so many things pointed towards it.

"What do you want me to do?" he asked the detective with a sigh.

"I want you to help me keep Fogg here until the warrant for his arrest arrives from London," Fix told him.

"Me! You want me to –"

"And I'll give you a share of the two thousand pounds reward."

"Never!" said Passepartout. He tried to get up but fell back on his chair, feeling his strength and his wits leaving him at the same time. "Monsieur Fix," he stammered, "even if everything you've told me is true . . . even if my master is the robber you're looking for . . . and I deny that he is . . . I'm his servant, and I've seen how good and generous he is . . . betray him? Never . . . no, not for all the gold in the world . . . I'd rather starve than do a thing like that!"

"You refuse?"

"I refuse."

"Then let's pretend I've said nothing to you," said Fix. "And let's have another drink."

"Yes, let's have another drink!"

Passepartout was becoming very drunk, and he knew it. And Fix knew that he must keep the Frenchman away from his master at all costs. He decided to finish the job. On the table were a few pipes filled with opium. Fix slipped one into Passepartout's hand. The Frenchman lit it, took a few puffs – and fell back without moving.

"At last!" said Fix. "Now Mr Fogg won't discover that the *Carnatic* is sailing tonight. And even if he does get away, at least he'll go without this cursed Frenchman!"

8

PHILEAS FOGG was not surprised when his servant did not appear at bedtime. He was not the sort of man to be surprised by anything. Besides, the steamer for Yokohama was not due to sail until the following morning, so he did not give it a thought.

The next morning, however, Passepartout did not appear when Mr Fogg rang for him. Mr Fogg then learned that his servant had not returned to the hotel the night before. Exactly what Phileas Fogg thought about this, no one could have said. He merely picked up his travelling bag and went with Aouda to a carriage which he had ordered.

When they got to the quay, Mr Fogg discovered that the *Carnatic* had sailed the evening before. He had expected to find both the steamer and his servant, now he had to do without both. But no sign of disappointment appeared on his face, and when Aouda looked at him anxiously, he merely said, "A trifling incident, Madam, no more."

Inspector Fix had been watching them from nearby. He came across.

"Were you not a passenger, like myself, on the *Rangoon* which arrived yesterday, sir?" said Fix.

"Yes," replied Mr Fogg, in a cool voice.

"Excuse me, but I expected to find your servant here."

"Do you know where he is, sir?" Aouda asked eagerly.

"Isn't he with you?" said Fix, pretending to be surprised.

"No," replied Aouda. "We haven't seen him since yesterday. Do you think he sailed on the *Carnatic* without us?"

"Without you, Madam?" said the detective. "Pardon the question, but did you intend to sail on that steamer?"

"Yes, sir."

"So did I, and I'm very disappointed. The *Carnatic* completed her repairs and left twelve hours earlier than expected, without telling anyone. Now we shall have to wait a week for the next boat."

As he said the words 'a week' Fix felt his heart leap for joy. A week! Fogg kept in Hong Kong for a week! That, surely, would be time enough for the warrant to arrive.

"But there are other ships in Hong Kong harbour," said Phileas Fogg, in his usual calm voice. And he and Aouda set off towards the docks.

Fix was horrified.

For three hours, Phileas Fogg searched the harbour from end to end, determined to charter a boat to take him to Yokohama, but all the vessels he saw were either loading or unloading, and thus were unable to sail.

Fix began to hope again.

Mr Fogg was not discouraged. He would go as far as Macao to find a ship if he had to. But then a sailor stopped him.

"Are you looking for a boat?" the sailor asked.

"Have you one ready to sail?" asked Mr Fogg.

"Yes, sir, a pilot boat. Number 43, the best boat in the harbour."

"She sails fast?"

"Between eight and nine knots. Would you like to see it?"

"Yes," said Mr Fogg.

"You will be pleased with it. Do you want to go for a trip?"

"No, a voyage."

"A voyage?" The sailor looked surprised.

"Will you take me to Yokohama?" asked Mr Fogg.

The sailor stared. "Are you joking, sir?"

"No. I missed the *Carnatic*, and I have to be in Yokohama by the 14th at the latest, to catch the steamer to San Francisco."

"I'm sorry," said the pilot, "but it's impossible."

"I'll pay you one hundred pounds a day, and a bonus of two hundred pounds if I get there in time," said Phileas Fogg.

"Are you serious?"

"Quite serious."

The pilot looked out to sea, torn between the desire to earn a large sum of money and the fear of venturing so far.

Fix held his breath.

"Well, pilot?" said Mr Fogg.

"Well, sir," the pilot replied, "I couldn't risk either my men or myself, or you either, on such a long voyage on so small a boat, and at this time of year. Besides, it's 1650 miles from Hong Kong to Yokohama, and we wouldn't get there in time."

"Only 1600 miles," corrected Mr Fogg.

"It comes to the same thing."

Fix breathed again.

"But," added the pilot, "there might be another way of managing it."

"How?" asked Phileas Fogg.

"By going to Shanghai, just eight hundred miles away. The route wouldn't take us so far from the Chinese coast, and that would be a great advantage as the currents run northwards."

"It's at Yokohama that I have to catch the steamer to San Fancisco," said Mr Fogg, "not Shanghai."

"Why?" said the pilot. "The San Francisco steamer *calls* at Yokohama, but it *starts* at Shanghai."

"Are you sure?"

"Certain."

"And when does the boat leave Shanghai?"

"On the 11th, at seven in the evening," said the pilot. "So we've got four days to get there. If the sea stays calm and the wind stays in the south-east, we can be there in time."

"When can you be ready to start?" asked Mr Fogg.

"In an hour."

"Right. Are you the captain of the boat?"

"Yes, sir. I'm John Bunsby, master of the *Tankadere*."

Mr Fogg paid him two hundred pounds in advance, then asked Fix if he wanted to accompany them. Fix, stunned by what had happened, thanked

him and said yes. Aouda was more concerned about Passepartout.

"I will do all I can for him," Phileas Fogg told her.

And while Fix, fuming with rage, went to find the pilot boat, the other two went to Hong Kong police station. Here Mr Fogg gave a description of Passepartout and left enough money to send him back to Europe. He did the same at the French Consulate. Then, after calling at the hotel to collect the luggage, he and Aouda went off to the boat.

At three o'clock, pilot boat number 43 was ready to sail. Mr Fogg and Aouda gave one last glance at the quay to see if there was any sign of Passepartout. Fix looked anxiously as well. He did not want the Frenchman turning up, there would be too many awkward explanations if he did. But Passepartout did not come, and at last John Bunsby steered the *Tankadere* towards the open sea, the wind filling its sails.

An eight hundred mile voyage in so small a schooner was a dangerous venture, especially at that time of year when the China seas were usually rough. But John Bunsby had faith in the *Tankadere*, and the little boat rose to the waves like a seagull.

Later in the day, they passed through the channels leading out of Hong Kong, and into the open sea. Later still, night came. The moon, now entering its first quarter, gave only a dim light which would soon be lost in the mists on the horizon. Clouds rose from the east.

Fix, in the bows, was deep in thought. He was certain Mr Fogg would not stop at Yokohama but would immediately take the steamer for San Francisco. In large a country like America, Phileas Fogg would feel safe. It had been a cunning plan. Instead of sailing straight from England to America, like any common criminal. Fogg had covered three-quarters of the earth to throw the police off his trail. But Fix would never leave him in peace. He would get an extradition order and take Fogg back to England.

But one thing had been accomplished. Fix had separated Passepartout from his master. And after what Fix had told Passepartout, it was essential that master and servant should never meet again.

Phileas Fogg was also thinking about his servant. Had there been a misunderstanding? Had Passepartout boarded the *Carnatic* at the last moment? Perhaps he had, and they would meet again at Yokohama.

By sunrise on 8th November, the schooner had sailed more than a hundred miles. With every sail taking the wind, the *Tankadere* was making the best possible speed.

That day, the police inspector spoke privately to Mr Fogg. "Sir, it was kind of you to offer me a place on the ship, but I insist on paying my share –"

"Do not let us discuss that, sir," replied Mr Fogg.

"But I insist –"

"No, sir," repeated Mr Fogg. "This will go down in my general expenses."

Fix said no more.

During that night, the *Tankadere* entered the Fo-Kien Straits, which separated Formosa from the Chinese coast, and they crossed the Tropic of Cancer. The sea was very rough, and at daybreak the wind increased. The look of the sky suggested an approaching gale.

"May I speak freely, sir?" the pilot said to Mr Fogg.

"Yes," replied Phileas Fogg.

"Well, we're in for a squall."

"Will it come from the north or the south?" was all Mr Fogg asked.

"From the south. Look there's a typhoon coming up!"

"I don't mind a typhoon from the south," said Mr Fogg. "It will help us on our way."

The pilot advised his passengers to go below, but none of them would leave the deck. They did not want to be imprisoned in a small space, almost without air, and be tossed about by the waves. At eight o'clock the rain fell and the *Tankadere* was swept along like a feather in the strongest wind the passengers had ever known. Throughout the day, the vessel scudded northwards, pushed by the enormous waves, and several times was almost overwhelmed by mountains of water.

At times the passengers were drenched with spray. Fix cursed, but a courageous Aouda watched Mr Fogg, who gave the impression that the typhoon was just part of his programme.

With nightfall the storm grew even more violent and it was a miracle that the little schooner did not capsize. Aouda was utterly exhausted, but she never complained, and more than once Mr Fogg had to rush over to protect her against the violence of the waves.

At daylight, the wind changed to the south-east – a favourable change, as the *Tankadere* was swept forward. From time to time the coast came into sight but there was no other vessel to be seen. The *Tankadere* was the only one still at sea. By noon the wind began to drop, and continued to do so as the afternoon went on. At last the passengers were able to take a little food and get some rest.

By the following morning, the 11th, John Bunsby was able to announce that they were less than a hundred miles from Shanghai. But with only one day in which to cover them! Mr Fogg had to reach Shanghai that very evening if he did not want to miss the steamer for Yokohama.

By noon, the *Tankadere* was forty-five miles from Shanghai. Six hours to reach the harbour before the steamer for Yokohama set out! The crew became anxious, and everyone – except Phileas Fogg, no doubt – felt his heart beating with impatience.

At six o'clock, John Bunsby reckoned they were only ten miles from the mouth of the Shanghai River, the town being twelve miles upstream. At seven o'clock they were still three miles from Shanghai. The pilot swore as he saw a bonus of two hundred pounds escaping him. Mr Fogg seemed as calm as ever, even though his whole fortune was at stake at that very moment.

A tall black shape, crowned by a plume of smoke, appeared on the horizon. It was the American steamer, leaving Shanghai.

"Curse it!" shouted John Bunsby.

"Signal her!" was all that Phileas Fogg said.

A small bronze cannon stood on the foredeck of the *Tankadere*, which was used to make signals in foggy weather. The cannon was loaded.

"Fire!" said Mr Fogg.

And the explosion of the little cannon echoed across the water.

9

AFTER LEAVING Hong Kong on 7th November at half-past six in the evening, the *Carnatic* cruised at full steam towards Japan. Though she was fully loaded with cargo and passengers, two cabins were empty. They were cabins which had been booked in the name of Phileas Fogg.

The following morning, when the steamer was 150 miles from Hong Kong, a passenger with a dazed look in his eye, and a shaky step, emerged from a second class cabin. It was Passepartout. He gulped down great breaths of sea air, which helped to sober him up, and then he began to collect his thoughts. Slowly, he remembered the events of the previous evening . . .

After Fix had left the opium bar, two attendants had picked up Passepartout and put him on the bed reserved for the opium smokers. Three hours later, Passepartout woke up, struggling against the stupefying effects of the drug. He knew there was something he had to do. Something important. Moments later, he was stumbling out of the bar shouting, "The *Carnatic*! The *Carnatic*!"

The boat had been at the quayside, ready to leave, and Passepartout had rushed up the gangway, staggered on to the deck – only to fall down unconscious just as the *Carnatic* was casting off. A few sailors, used to this sort of thing, had carried the poor fellow down into the second class cabin.

It was the same cabin from which now, the morning after, Passepartout had just emerged.

'I haven't missed the boat,' he thought thankfully. 'But what will Mr Fogg say?' His thoughts moved on to Fix. 'I hope we see no more of him. After what he asked me to do, he won't have dared follow me on to the *Carnatic*. A police inspector! A detective, following Mr Fogg and accusing him of robbing the Bank of England! Rubbish! Mr Fogg is no more a thief than I am a murderer!'

Should he explain all this to his master? Ought he to tell him about the part Fix was playing in this affair? Or would it be better to wait until they got back to London before telling him that an agent of the Metropolitan Police had followed him round the world? Then they could enjoy the joke together. Yes, that might be best. Anyway, the first thing to do was to find Monsieur Fogg and apologise. Passepartout felt badly about his behaviour the previous evening.

He saw nobody on deck who looked like his master or Aouda. But it was still early, so he assumed Aouda was still sleeping and Mr Fogg was playing whist with somebody, as usual. But when he went down to the saloon, Monsieur Fogg was not there. The only thing to do was to ask the purser which cabin Monsieur Fogg was in, but the purser replied that he did not know of any passenger with that name.

Passepartout described his master, saying that there was a young lady with him.

"We have no lady on board," said the purser. "Here's the passenger list,

you can see for yourself."

Passepartout read through the list and saw that his master's name was not there. "I am on the *Carnatic*, I suppose?" he said.

"Yes," answered the purser.

"Going to Yokohama?"

"That's right."

For a moment Passepartout had been afraid he was on the wrong boat. Then the truth dawned on him. The sailing time of the *Carnatic* had been changed and he was supposed to have told Monsieur Fogg! But he hadn't! So it was his fault that Monsieur Fogg and Aouda had missed the boat! But it was even more the fault of the traitorous Inspector Fix who had tricked Passepartout. Now Monsieur Fogg was ruined, he had lost his bet, and might even have been arrested and thrown in jail!

After the first shock of what he had done began to pass, Passepartout began to consider his own position. It was not good, he realised. Here he was, on his way to Japan. But how would he get back? He had no money. Luckily, his meals and cabin had been paid for in advance, so he had five or six days in which to decide what to do.

On the 13th, with the morning tide, the *Carnatic* entered Yokohama harbour. It moored alongside the quay, and Passepartout went ashore. He wandered haphazardly through the streets, which swarmed with people of all races – Americans, English, Chinese, Dutch – and with merchants willing to buy or sell anything.

Passepartout considered going to the French or English consuls but shrank from the idea of having to tell his story. He would do this only if all else failed, he decided.

At night, the streets were lit with multi-coloured lanterns. A weary Passepartout made his way through them. He watched the acrobats performing their amazing feats, and the astrologers who were collecting crowds around their telescopes. He was tired and hungry.

The next day, he decided that at all costs he must get something to eat, and the sooner the better. Admittedly, he could always sell his watch, but he would rather have died of hunger. Now, if ever, was the time to use his strong, if not very muscial, voice. He knew a few French and English tunes and he decided to try them.

But it was still a little early, he thought. Then it occurred to him that he was a bit too well dressed for a strolling artist, and he got the idea of changing his clothes to others more suitable. And by doing so, he might be able to get a little money to buy food.

After a long search, he discovered an old clothes dealer, and explained his needs. Some time later, Passepartout left the shop wearing an old Japanese robe and a faded turban – and with some money jingling in his pocket.

He found a modest-looking teahouse and bought himself some breakfast. Then he had the idea offering his services as a cook or steward on one of the steamers leaving for America, in return for a free passage and food. Once in San Francisco, Passepartout was sure he could find a way out of his difficulties. The main thing was to cross those 4700 miles of ocean which lay

between Japan and the New World.

Passepartout made for the harbour. But the nearer he got, the sillier his idea began to seem. Why should they need a steward or cook on an American ship, and who would employ him dressed up as he was? What references could he give?

As these thoughts were passing through his head, Passepartout saw a man dressed as a clown. The clown was carrying a placard through the streets, and it read:

William Batulcar's
Troupe of Japanese Acrobats
——

Last Performances
Before Their Departure for the United States
of the
Long, Long Noses
Come and see this Great Attraction
——

"The United States of America!" exclaimed Passepartout. "Just what I'm looking for!" And he followed the clown back to a large theatre where a troupe of contortionists, jugglers, clowns and acrobats were to give their last performance before leaving Japan.

Passepartout asked to see Monsieur Batulcar, who appeared in person.

"What do you want?" the man asked Passepartout.

"Do you want a servant?" asked Passepartout.

"A servant!" exclaimed Batulcar, stroking his goatee beard. "I already have two." He looked closely at Passepartout. "You're not Japanese! Why are you dressed like that?"

"One dresses as well as one can," replied Passepartout.

"True enough. You're a Frenchman, aren't you?"

"Yes, from Paris."

"Then you must know how to make funny faces?"

Passepartout said that he could.

"Are you strong?" asked Batulcar.

"I am."

"And can you sing?"

"Yes," answered Passepartout.

"But can you sing standing on your head?"

"I certainly can," replied Passepartout.

Batulcar agreed to give him a job.

The performance was due to start at three o'clock and men, women and children were rushing to take their places on the narrow benches and in the boxes facing the stage.

They watched with delight as the acrobats and jugglers performed their marvellous tricks, all carried out with remarkable precision. But the main attraction of the whole performance was the display by the Long Noses, astonishing acrobats as yet unknown in Europe. What made them different from the others were the long noses which they wore on their faces. These 61

noses were made from bamboo canes five or six or ten feet long, some straight, others curved. It was on these bamboo noses, which were securely fastened, that they performed their balancing feats – the most spectacular of which was the human pyramid. Instead of climbing on one another's shoulders, they used nothing but their noses!

One of the performers who helped to form the base of the pyramid had left the troupe and, as all that was needed was strength and skill, Passepartout had been put in his place. With a six foot bamboo nose strapped to his face, Passepartout took his place amongst those making the base of the pyramid. They all lay flat on their backs, noses pointing into the air, and a second batch of acrobats took up their positions on the noses. A third batch placed themselves above these, then a fourth, and so on until the pyramid reached to the very top of the theatre.

Just as the applause was increasing, the whole pyramid suddenly tottered . . . and collapsed!

The fault was Passepartout's. Leaving his position, he had leapt across the footlights and clambered up to the right hand gallery.

"Oh, my master!" he cried. "My master!"

"Is it you?"

"Yes, it's me!" cried Passepartout.

"Very well! In that case my lad, come along to the steamer!"

Mr Fogg, Aouda, who was with him, and Passepartout rushed down the corridors. But outside the hall they found a furious Mr Batulcar, shouting and demanding damages.

Phileas Fogg calmed Batulcar's fury by throwing him a handful of banknotes. And at half-past six, just as it was about to sail, Fogg and Aouda set foot on the American steamer, followed by Passepartout, the six-foot nose still strapped to his face!

What had happened off Shanghai is easy to understand. The *Tankadere*'s signals had been sighted from the Yokohama steamer, and the captain had steered towards the little schooner. Phileas Fogg then paid John Bunsby the agreed sum for his passage and, accompanied by Aouda and Fix, had climbed aboard the steamer.

It arrived at Yokohama on the morning of 14th November. Phileas Fogg left Fix to go about his business and went aboard the *Carnatic*. There he learned that Passepartout had indeed arrived at Yokohama the previous day.

Mr Fogg, who had to leave for San Francisco that evening, set out in search of his servant. He went to the French and English consuls, then roamed the streets with Aouda, gradually beginning to despair of ever finding Passepartout.

It was sheer chance that took them into Mr Batulcar's theatre. Mr Fogg would never have recognised Passepartout at the bottom of the pyramid, but Passepartout had seen him at once.

It was Aouda who told Passepartout of the journey from Hong Kong in the company of a certain Mr Fix. At the mention of Mr Fix, Passepartout did not bat an eyelid. He did not think the time had yet come to tell his master what had passed between the detective and himself. Instead, he blamed only himself for his adventures in the Hong Kong opium bar.

Mr Fogg listened coldly and without comment. Then he gave Passepartout money to go and buy some more suitable clothes to wear on the journey to America.

10

THE STEAMER crossing from Yokohama to San Francisco was called the *General Grant*. It was a huge paddle steamer, well equipped and very fast. Travelling at twelve knots, it would not take more than three weeks to cross the Pacific, arriving at San Francisco on 2nd December. If all went well, Phileas Fogg would be in New York on the 11th and London on the 20th – a few hours earlier than the all-important 21st December.

Mr Fogg was as calm and as quiet as ever, but Aouda's feelings of gratitude towards him were growing into something rather more like love, although Mr Fogg seemed quite unmoved by them. Aouda often chatted with Passepartout, who had guessed her feelings for his master and who never got tired of praising Phileas Fogg's honesty, generosity and kindness.

Nine days after leaving Yokohama, on the 23rd November, they had journeyed round exactly one half of the globe, although they had really covered more than two-thirds of the whole distance because of the roundabout way they had been forced to go – London to Aden, Aden to Bombay, Calcutta to Singapore, Singapore to Yokohama. But from now on their course was a straight one.

Also on 23rd November, Passepartout's watch, which he had refused to alter to local time, now actually agreed with the ship's clock. But if the dial of his watch had been divided into *twenty-four hours* instead of twelve, its hands would have shown nine in the evening (or twenty-one o'clock) and not nine in the morning.

And where was Inspector Fix at this moment?

He was, in fact, on the *General Grant*.

When they had reached Yokohama, the detective had left Mr Fogg and gone straight to the British Consulate. There he had at last found the warrant which had been following him from Bombay, and which was already forty days old. Unhappily, it was useless! Mr Fogg had left British soil, and now an extradition order would be needed to arrest him.

"Very well," thought Fix, after his first explosion of anger. "My warrant isn't any good here, but it will be in England. I'll follow him there. As for the money, I hope to heaven some of it is left!"

He was already aboard the *General Grant* when Mr Fogg and Aouda arrived with Passepartout. Fix was horrified to see Passepartout and immediately hid in his cabin, hoping to keep out of his enemy's sight during the trip.

But on such a long voyage, he could not succeed. One morning he found himself face to face with Passepartout on the foredeck. Without a word, Passepartout flew at Fix's throat and gave the detective a beating.

Fix struggled to his feet afterwards. "Have you finished?"

"Yes, for the time being," said Passepartout.

"Then come and have a word with me, for the sake of your master."

Passepartout followed him and they both sat down.

"You've given me a beating," said Fix, "and I expected it. But now listen to me. So far I've been against Mr Fogg, but now I'm on his side."

"So now you think he's an honest man?" said Passepartout.

"No, but as Mr Fogg seems to be going back to London, I'll do all I can to help him get there. It's in my interest, you see. And in yours, I might add, for only in England will you be able to find out for certain whether you're in the service of a criminal or an honest man!"

Passepartout had to admit the sense of what Fix was saying.

"Are we friends?" asked the detective.

"Friends, no," replied Passepartout. "Allies, yes. But at the slightest sign of treachery I'll wring your neck."

"Agreed," said Fix, quietly.

Eleven days later, on 3rd December, the *General Grant* arrived at San Francisco. So far, Mr Fogg had neither gained nor lost a single day.

The train for New York was due to leave at six o'clock that evening. Mr Fogg had the whole day to spend in the Californian city. After breakfast at a hotel, he and Aouda went to the British Consulate to have Mr Fogg's passport stamped with a visa. Passepartout suggested that it might be wise for them to buy revolvers as they were about to travel through Indian country where they could be attacked. Mr Fogg said he thought this unnecessary but that Passepartout could go and buy some if he liked.

Philéas Fogg had hardly walked a hundred yards when he met Fix. The detective pretended to be surprised.

"You mean we crossed the Pacific together but never met on board!" said Fix. "Well, how nice to meet you again. I am going back to Europe and it will be an honour to continue my journey in such pleasant company."

Mr Fogg replied politely that the honour would be his.

Moments later, Phileas Fogg, Aouda and Fix found themselves in the midst **67**

of a huge crowd. Some people were shouting "Hurrah for Kamerfield!" and others "Hurrah for Mandiboy!" It was a political meeting, and everyone was getting very excited. Banners were waved. Cheers and insults grew louder, and a fight broke out.

Mr Fogg and Fix tried to protect Aouda but were roughly jostled. A huge, broad-shouldered man with a red beard and an even redder face raised a fist against Mr Fogg and would have injured him badly if Fix had not stepped in the way, taking the full force of the blow.

"Yankee!" said Mr Fogg, glaring at his opponent.

"Limey!" replied the other. "We'll meet again."

"Whenever you like."

"What's your name?"

"Phileas Fogg. And yours?"

"Colonel Stamp Proctor."

After this, the crowd swept onwards. Fix was knocked over, but got up again. Mr Fogg thanked him.

"Don't mention it," said Fix, "but we must buy some new clothes."

As a result of the fight their clothes had been torn to pieces, but an hour later, wearing new clothes, they went back to the hotel.

Passepartout was waiting there with six revolvers. Aouda explained what had happened and Passepartout realised that Fix was indeed keeping his word, and that he was no longer an enemy.

11

NEW YORK and San Francisco were linked by 3,786 miles of railway. Between Omaha and the Pacific it crossed a region inhabited by wild beasts and Indians. The whole journey would take seven days, which meant Phileas Fogg could catch the Liverpool steamer from New York on 11th December.

The train left Oakland station at six. It was already cold and dark, and there was little conversation in Phileas Fogg's carriage. Later, whilst they slept, the train hurtled at full speed across California.

The following day they saw large numbers of buffaloes which, by crossing the railway line in their thousands, forced the train to wait until it was clear to go on again. Phileas Fogg remained calm, but Passepartout was furious at the delay.

"What a country!" he exclaimed. "Trains stopped by cattle!"

Bad weather also worried him. By 7th December they had reached Green River station, and during the night there had been a heavy fall of snow. It did not slow the train down, but Passepartout complained about the madness of travelling in winter.

A few passengers got out and walked up and down the platform at Green River. Aouda recognised one of them. It was Colonel Stamp Proctor.

When the train started again and Mr Fogg was dozing, Aouda whispered to Fix and Passepartout, "That man Proctor is on the train!"

"Don't worry," said Fix. "I was the one he insulted the most. It will be me he has to deal with."

Aouda shook her head. "Mr Fogg will insist on avenging his honour. We must make sure he doesn't see him."

It was decided that the best way to do this was to keep Mr Fogg occupied by playing his favourite card game of whist.

It was early afternoon when, after three loud whistles, the train stopped. Passepartout jumped down from the carriage to go and investigate. The train had stopped in front of a red signal, and the driver and guard were talking with a track-watchman who had been sent from Medicine Bow to meet the train. Some passengers had joined in the discussion and one of them was Colonel Stamp Proctor.

"There's no way of going on," the watchman was saying. "The bridge at Medicine Bow is shaky and it can't take the weight of the train."

"We're not going to stay here and take root in the snow!" protested Colonel Proctor.

"They've telegraphed to Omaha station for a train," said the guard, "but it won't reach Medicine Bow for another six hours."

"Six hours!" cried Passepartout.

"It will take us that time to reach the station anyway," said the guard. "It's twelve miles away on the other side of the river."

"Twelve miles on foot, in the snow!" exclaimed the Colonel.

"There must be some way of getting over the bridge with the train," said the driver. "Perhaps if I drive at full speed . . ."

"What a crazy idea!" said Passepartout.

But some of the passengers wanted to try it, especially Colonel Proctor. Passepartout could not understand them.

"There's a simpler way," he began.

"Let's not waste time talking," somebody said.

"A few minutes thought –"

"The driver is certain we can get across."

"I don't doubt it," said Passepartout, "but –"

"Are you scared?" Colonel Proctor asked him.

"Me, scared!" cried Passepartout. "Certainly not!"

"All aboard!" shouted the guard.

"Yes, all aboard," said Passepartout. "But I can't help thinking it would have been better for us to cross the bridge on foot first and the train next!" But nobody heard these wise words.

Everyone went back to their carriages and, after a blast on the whistle, the train reversed back nearly a mile before moving forward again. Faster and faster it went, until it reached a terrifying hundred miles an hour! Nobody saw anything of the bridge. The train seemed to leap from one bank to the other!

But it had hardly crossed the river when the bridge, completely destroyed, fell with a roar into the rapids of Medicine Bow.

70   That evening the train reached the highest point of the journey, 8,091 feet

above sea level. Now it had only to descend to the Atlantic, across boundless plains. In three days and three nights the travellers had covered 1,382 miles from San Francisco, and another four days and four nights should bring them to New York.

The following day, Phileas Fogg and his friends were playing whist when Mr Fogg heard a voice behind him.

"If I were you, I'd play a diamond." It was Colonel Proctor.

Phileas Fogg looked up, and the two men recognised one another.

"So it's you, Mister Limey!" the colonel exclaimed. "It's you who wants to play a spade!"

"And I am playing it," said Mr Fogg, putting down the card.

Colonel Proctor tried to snatch it up. "You don't know anything about this game," he said.

"Perhaps I'd be better at another," said Phileas Fogg, standing up.

"You have only to try!" said the other.

Suddenly, both men heard the sound of savage yells and gunfire. Mixed with these were cries of terror from inside the carriages.

The train was being attacked by Indians!

It was not the first attack by the daring Sioux Indians, they had held up trains more than once and knew the best way of going about it. They had jumped on to the footboards of the moving train and had clambered into the carriages and on to the roof. A Sioux chief, wanting to stop the engine, had jumped on, half-killed the driver and fireman, but then had mistakenly *opened* the throttle instead of shutting it.

Now the train was rushing forward at full speed.

Most of the passengers carried guns and defended themselves bravely. Aouda, revolver in hand, fired through broken windows whenever one of the savages appeared. Colonel Proctor and Phileas Fogg, both clutching revolvers, made their way towards the front carriages where the shots and explosions were loudest.

Several passengers were badly wounded and were lying on the seats.

Fort Kearney station was only two miles ahead, and there were American soldiers there. But if the train went beyond Fort Kearney, then it would be in the hands of the Indians before it reached the next station.

The guard was fighting at Mr Fogg's side when a bullet brought him down. As he fell, he cried, "If the train doesn't stop within five minutes, we're done for!"

"I'll stop it," said Phileas Fogg, getting ready to rush out of the carriage.

"Stay here, Monsieur!" shouted Passepartout. "This is my business."

Passepartout opened a door and managed to slip under the carriage without the Indians seeing him. Then, whilst bullets whizzed over his head, he worked his way forward under the carriages, using all the skills of his old acrobatic days. Then, hanging on with one hand between the luggage van and the engine, he used the other hand to unhook the safety chains. Luck was on his side for a sudden jolt of the engine jerked it free. Parted from the tender, the train gradually fell behind while the engine raced ahead with increased speed.

The carriages finally came to a halt less than a hundred yards from Kearney station. There the soldiers from the fort, having heard the shooting, rushed up. The Sioux had not waited for them, and even before the train had stopped, all had run off.

But when the passengers were counted on the station platform, it was discovered that three were missing. One of these was Passepartout.

Had the three been killed in the fight? Were they prisoners of the Indians? No one knew. Many passengers were injured and one of the most seriously hurt was Colonel Proctor. He had fought bravely but had been brought down by a bullet in the stomach. He was carried into the station with others who needed immediate attention.

Aouda was safe, Phileas Fogg had escaped without a scratch, but Fix had been hit in the arm, although his wound was not serious. But Passepartout was missing and tears were streaming down Aouda's face.

"I shall find him, dead or alive," Mr Fogg said quietly to her.

"Oh, Mr Fogg!" cried the young woman.

"Alive, provided we do not waste a single moment."

With this decision, Phileas Fogg gave up all chance of catching the steamer at New York. And he looked like getting no help from the army.

"This fort is my responsibility," the captain told him. "I cannot leave it."

"Sir," said Phileas Fogg. "Three men's lives are at stake."

"I cannot risk the lives of fifty to save three," said the captain.

"Very well," said Mr Fogg. "I shall go by myself! Every passenger on the train owes his life to one of those men."

The captain sighed. "You can't go alone," he said at last. He turned to his men. "I want thirty volunteers to go with this brave man."

Every man stepped forward, and the captain had to choose thirty.

"Thank you, Captain," said Mr Fogg.

"Will you let me come with you?" asked Fix.

"You can do as you please," said Phileas Fogg. "But if you really want to help, you'll stay with this lady in case anything happens to me."

The police inspector's face became pale. Should he part from this man whom he had followed so persistently? Should he let him go off into the wilderness? He stared into Mr Fogg's calm, honest face.

"I'll stay," said Fix.

Mr Fogg gave Aouda his precious travelling bag. Then he told the soldiers, "My friends, there will be a thousand pounds for you if we save those prisoners." And they all rode off.

It was a few minutes after midday.

Aouda waited in a room at the station, thinking about Mr Fogg's calm courage and how he had sacrificed his fortune and put his life in danger, all without any fuss. Inspector Fix paced impatiently on the platform outside. Now that Fogg had gone, he cursed himself for being so stupid.

"He's gone and he won't come back!" Fix muttered. "I'm an idiot!"

At two o'clock, while the snow was falling heavily, long whistle blasts were heard from the east. Yet no train was expected. Help summoned by telegraph could not have arrived so soon, and the train from Omaha to San Francisco was not due until the following day.

The mystery was soon explained.

It was the engine which had been detached from the train. It had travelled on several miles before the fire burned low and it ran out of steam. An hour later, after gradually slowing down, it had come to a stop about twenty miles from Kearney station. The driver and fireman were not dead, and after recovering consciousness and realising what must have happened, they had brought the train back.

The passengers were delighted, for now they would be able to continue their journey.

But Aouda went to the guard. "Are you going to leave?" she asked.

"At once, Madam," said the guard.

"But what about those poor prisoners?"

"We can't wait," said the guard. "We're already three hours late."

"When will the next train be coming from San Francisco?"

"Tomorrow evening, Madam," answered the guard.

"But that will be too late! You *must* wait!"

"Impossible. If you want to go, take your seat."

"I'll not go," said Aouda.

Fix heard this. Moments earlier, he had planned to go with the train, but now he decided to stay. The passengers – including Colonel Proctor – boarded the train. The driver blew the whistle and the train moved off, its white smoke mingling with the whirling snowflakes.

The hours went by. Evening came and Mr Fogg and the soldiers had not returned. Where were they? Had they been able to catch up with the Indians? Or were they lost?

With night the snow fell less thickly, and at dawn a pale sun rose above this misty horizon. Then, at seven o'clock, some shots rang out. And there, half a mile away, they saw a small band of men returning. Mr Fogg was marching at their head, and with him were Passepartout and the two other travellers who had been snatched by the Sioux.

There had been a fight with the Indians ten miles south of Fort Kearney. Passepartout and his fellow prisoners had been battling with their captors only moments before the soldiers came rushing to their help.

Both rescued and rescuers were greeted with shouts of joy.

Phileas Fogg paid the soldiers their reward, and Passepartout said, "I'm costing my master a pretty penny!" He looked round for the train.

"It's gone," Fix told him.

"And when will the next train come along?" asked Phileas Fogg.

"Not until this evening."

"Ah," was all Mr Fogg replied.

He was now twenty hours behind time, and Passepartout was in despair. It was all his fault! But then Fix walked up to Mr Fogg.

"Seriously, sir," he said, "are you in a great hurry?"

"I am," replied Mr Fogg.

"If your journey hadn't been interrupted by those Indians, you would have got to New York as early as the morning of the 11th, yes?"

"Yes, twelve hours before the departure of the Liverpool steamer."

"You are twenty hours late," said Fix. "The difference between twenty and

twelve is eight. Eight hours to make up. Would you like to try?"

"On foot?" asked Mr Fogg.

"No," Fix replied. "On a sledge. A man has offered us the use of a sledge with sails."

Mr Fogg went to examine the strange-looking vehicle. It was built of wood and could carry five or six people. It ran on wooden runners and there was a tall mast with a sail. At the stern was a sort of tiller to steer the machine.

Within a few moments, a bargain was struck between Mr Fogg and Mr Mudge, the owner of this land-yacht. And by eight o'clock, the sledge was speeding across the snow at forty miles an hour.

What a journey it was! Huddled together, the travellers could not speak for the cold. The sledge flew over the carpet of snow, Mudge at the helm, holding it on course. He had been promised a bonus if they arrived within the agreed time.

At noon they crossed the frozen River Platte, and an hour later arrived at Omaha station. Passepartout and Fix jumped off the sledge and helped Mr Fogg and Aouda down. Mr Fogg paid Mudge, including his bonus, and then they all rushed into the station.

There was an express train going to Chicago almost immediately, and Phileas Fogg and his companions had to run to catch it. Travelling at high speed, the train passed through Des Moines and Iowa City, then during the night crossed the Mississippi at Davenport. They arrived at Chicago at four o'clock in the afternoon of the 10th.

A further nine hundred miles separated them from New York, but there was no shortage of trains. They transferred to another which set off at full speed, as though it realised Mr Fogg had no time to lose.

And on 11th December, at 11.15 pm, the train pulled up at the station that was in front of the very pier where the Liverpool steamer, the *China*, should have been standing.

But it had left forty-five minutes earlier!

12

As it sailed away, the *China* seemed to have taken Phileas Fogg's last hopes with it. None of the other boats there could be of any use to him. The French boat, the *Pereire*, was not due to sail until the 14th, two days later, and the German boat did not sail directly to London or Liverpool. And one other boat, due to put to sea the next day, only used sails and not steam and would be too slow.

Passepartout blamed himself. He had never stopped putting obstacles in his master's path! But Phileas Fogg blamed nobody. He merely said, "We shall decide what to do tomorrow. Come along."

Mr Fogg, Aouda, Fix and Passepartout took rooms at the St Nicholas Hotel on Broadway. Phileas Fogg slept soundly, but his worried companions spent a restless night.

Next morning, Mr Fogg left the hotel alone. He told Passepartout to await his return, and to warn Aouda to be ready to leave at any moment. Then he went to the banks of the Hudson River and searched amongst the vessels moored to the quay or anchored in the river for any that were about to sail. In New York, not a day passed without a hundred vessels setting out for every part of the world. But most of them were sailing ships and of no use to Phileas Fogg.

Then he noticed a merchant steamer, its funnel giving out great puffs of smoke, ready to leave. The captain was on board and when Phileas Fogg asked to see him, he came at once.

"I'm Phileas Fogg of London," said Mr Fogg.

"And I'm Andrew Speedy of Cardiff," said the captain.

"You are about to sail?"

"In an hour."

"For where?"

"Bordeaux."

"Have you any passengers?"

"Never carry passengers, they're too troublesome. This is a cargo ship," said the captain.

"Your ship travels fast?"

"Between eleven and twelve knots. The *Henrietta*'s famous for that."

"Will you take me and three others to Liverpool?" said Mr Fogg.

"No, I'm going to Bordeaux."

"No matter what I offer?"

"No matter what you offer."

"But the owner –"

"I'm the owner," said Andrew Speedy. "The ship belongs to me."

"I'll buy it from you," said Phileas Fogg.

"No."

Phileas Fogg did not bat an eyelid. "Well, will you take me to Bordeaux?" he asked.

"Not even if you paid me two hundred dollars."

"I'm offering you two thousand."

"For each person?"

"Yes," said Phileas Fogg.

"And there's four of you?"

"Four."

Captain Speedy scratched his head. Eight thousand dollars, and he didn't even have to change his course! At two thousand each, these passengers became valuable merchandise.

"I'm going at nine," he said.

"We'll be here," said Mr Fogg.

The next day, 13th December, a man went on to the bridge of the *Henrietta*. It was *not*, as might be supposed, Captain Speedy. It was Phileas Fogg. Captain Speedy was locked in his cabin, shouting and yelling at the top of his voice.

What had happened was very simple. Phileas Fogg wanted to go to Liverpool; the captain did not want to take him there. Then Phileas Fogg agreed to go to Bordeaux, but during the thirty hours that he had been on board, he had used his banknotes well and now the whole crew were taking orders from him. Which was why the *Henrietta* was heading for Liverpool and not Bordeaux.

How all this would end only time would tell, but Aouda felt uneasy about it, although she said nothing. Fix had been so astonished that he had said nothing. Secretly, he thought this man Fogg was a pirate and that the ship would not be going to Liverpool at all but to some part of the world where Fogg could hide. But Passepartout found the whole thing delightful and worked happily alongside the crew, his good humour spreading to everyone on board.

During the first few days the voyage went splendidly. The sea was not too rough, the sails were hoisted, and the *Henrietta* forged ahead. But on the 16th December, when the voyage was almost half over, the engineer came on deck to speak to Mr Fogg. A lively conversation followed. Passepartout began to feel vaguely anxious as he watched them. He caught a few words of what was being said.

"You are sure of what you're saying?" said Phileas Fogg.

"Certain, sir," replied the engineer. "Remember, we've been keeping all our furnaces going, and while we had enough coal to go from New York to Bordeaux under easy steam, we haven't enough to take us from New York to Liverpool at full speed."

"I will think it over," said Mr Fogg.

Now Passepartout understood what was wrong. The coal was running out! Well, if Phileas Fogg could cope with that, he would be a really great man, Passepartout thought.

That evening, Phileas Fogg sent for the engineer.

"Heap up the fires and carry on until the fuel runs out," he said.

So the steamer rushed on at full speed, its funnel pushing out clouds of thick smoke. But two days later, on the 18th, the engineer informed Mr Fogg that the coal would run out that day.

At noon, Passepartout was sent to fetch Captain Speedy.

"Where are we?" was the first thing the captain asked Phileas Fogg.

"Seven hundred and seventy miles from Liverpool," Mr Fogg replied calmly.

"Pirate!" yelled Andrew Speedy.

"I sent for you, sir, to ask you to sell me your ship . . ."

"No! By the devil no!"

". . . because I need to burn her."

"Burn my ship!"

"Yes – at least the upper part, for we're running out of fuel."

"Burn my ship!" spluttered Captain Speedy. "A ship worth fifty thousand dollars!"

"Here are sixty thousand," replied Phileas Fogg, offering the captain a roll of banknotes.

The captain suddenly forgot his anger. His ship was twenty years old, and this looked like being the opportunity of a lifetime.

"And the iron hull will be left to me?" he asked.

"The iron hull and the engine, sir. Done?"

"Done!" said Captain Speedy. And he seized the roll of banknotes.

Passepartout had turned white. Fix had almost collapsed with shock, for Phileas Fogg had just paid nearly twenty thousand pounds for the ship and he was going to let the vendor, Andrew Speedy keep the hull and the engine.

As Speedy pocketed the money, Mr Fogg said, "All this will not surprise you when I tell you that unless I am back in London on the 21st December at 8.45 pm, I shall lose twenty thousand pounds."

"Well, Captain Fogg," said Andrew Speedy, laughing, "there's something of the Yankee about you!" Which was the highest praise the American could think of giving Phileas Fogg.

Mr Fogg now gave orders for all the wooden fittings on the ship to be broken up and used as fuel. The poop deck, the deckhouses, the cabins and the berths – all were sacrificed. On the following day, the 19th, the masts, booms and spars were burned. On the 20th, the rails and the greater part of the deck were burned up. But on that day the Irish coast was sighted.

By 10 pm, however, the ship was still only passing Queenstown and Phileas Fogg had less than twenty-four hours to reach London. Yet this was the amount of time the *Henrietta* needed to get to Liverpool.

"Can we enter Queenstown harbour?" asked Mr Fogg.

"Not for three hours," said Captain Speedy. "Only at high tide."

"We shall wait," replied Mr Fogg, calmly, not letting his expression show that he had one last plan which he hoped would succeed.

Queenstown was a port on the Irish coast where the transatlantic liners from the United States unloaded their mailbags. The mail was sent on to Dublin by express train, and from Dublin crossed to Liverpool by fast steamers, getting there twelve hours before the fastest ships of the transatlantic lines.

Phileas Fogg hoped to do the same. Then, instead of reaching Liverpool the next evening on the *Henrietta*, he would be there at noon, leaving him enough time to get to London by 8.45 pm.

At one in the morning, Phileas Fogg shook hands with Captain Speedy and said goodbye. There was nothing left of the *Henrietta* except the hull and the engine, but it was still worth half the sum it had been sold for.

As they went ashore, Fix was tempted to arrest Phileas Fogg. Yet he did not do

83

so. Why? Had he changed his mind about Mr Fogg? Had he realised that he was mistaken?

Whatever the truth of the matter, Fix did not leave him.

They boarded the train at Queenstown at 1.30 am, reached Dublin at dawn, and at once got on a steamer heading for Liverpool. At twenty to twelve on 21st December, Phileas Fogg finally landed on the quay at Liverpool, six hours from London.

But at that moment Fix went up to him. He put a hand on Mr Fogg's shoulder, and showing him a warrant, said, "You really are Mr Phileas Fogg?"

"Yes," replied Mr Fogg.

"Then in the Queen's name, I arrest you!"

13

PHILEAS FOGG was in prison. He was locked up in the Custom House cells and was to spend the night there before being taken to London. He was well and truly ruined, and just as he had been about to reach his goal. He sat motionless in his cell, not showing any sign of anger and still perfectly calm. He had placed his watch on a table and was carefully following the movement of its hands.

The Custom House clock struck one, and Mr Fogg noticed that his watch was two minutes fast by that clock.

Two o'clock came. If he could board an express train now he could still reach London and the Reform Club by 8.45 pm.

At thirty-three minutes past two his cell door opened and he saw Aouda, Passepartout and Fix rushing towards him.

Fix was out of breath. "Sir!" he gasped. "Forgive me . . . a mistake . . . somebody who resembled you . . . robber arrested three days ago . . . you're free!"

Phileas Fogg was free! He went up to the detective and made the only sudden movement he would ever make in his life – he hit Fix with both fists!

"Well hit!" cried Passepartout.

Fix, lying on the floor, did not say a word. But Mr Fogg, Aouda and Passepartout quickly left the Custom House, jumped into a cab, and in a few minutes arrived at Liverpool station.

Phileas Fogg asked if there was an express train about to leave for London, but the express had gone thirty-five minutes before. He then ordered a special train and, at three o'clock, they set off for London.

He had to cover the distance in five hours – something which is quite possible when the whole of the line is clear. But that day it wasn't and there were unavoidable delays. By the time they arrived in the city, all the clocks were pointing to 8.50 pm.

After completing his journey around the world, Phileas Fogg had arrived five minutes late!

He had lost.

After leaving the station, Phileas Fogg told Passepartout to buy some food, and

then went home. He was ruined. And all because of that blundering fool of an inspector. Out of the large sum of money Mr Fogg had taken with him, only a few pounds remained. And the twenty-thousand pounds which was in his bank he now owed to his friends at the Reform Club.

The night went by. Aouda had been given a room in the house in Savile Row but she did not sleep well. From certain words Mr Fogg had spoken, she was afraid he might be about to put an end to his life.

Passepartout also kept a close watch on his master. First of all, however, he went up to his own room and turned off the gas, which had been burning for eighty days.

The next day, Phileas Fogg's neighbours in Savile Row would have been very surprised to learn that Mr Fogg had returned home, for all the windows and doors were still shut tight. For the first time since he had lived here, Mr Fogg did not go to the Reform Club when the clock struck eleven. There was no need. His fellow members were not waiting there for him now. The previous day, that fateful date of Saturday 21st December, Phileas Fogg had failed to appear at the Reform Club at 8.45 pm, and he had lost his bet. There was not even a need for him to go to his bank and draw out the money. His friends held a cheque which he had signed.

So Mr Fogg did not have to go out, and he stayed in his room and put his affairs in order. All day, Passepartout went up and down the stairs, listening outside Mr Fogg's room, even peering through the keyhole, and fearing some dreadful catastrophe at any moment.

At seven-thirty in the evening, Mr Fogg went to see Aouda in her room. He sat down in a chair near the fireplace and was silent for five long minutes. Then he looked up at Aouda and said, "Madam, please forgive me for bringing you to England."

"But, Mr Fogg –"

"Please allow me to finish," continued Mr Fogg. "When I had the idea of taking you far from that country of yours which had become so dangerous for you, I was a rich man. I intended to offer you part of my fortune so that your life would have been free and happy. Now I am ruined."

"I know that, Mr Fogg," replied the young woman. "And now I must ask you to forgive me for accompanying you, and perhaps being part of the cause of your ruin by delaying you."

"You could not have stayed in India," said Mr Fogg. "I could only be sure of your safety by taking you with me. I hope you will now allow me to give you what little money I have left."

"But what about you, Mr Fogg?" asked Aouda.

"I do not need anything," Phileas Fogg replied.

"But you must have friends who can help you."

"I have no friends."

"Your relatives –"

"I have no relatives left."

"Then I am sorry for you, Mr Fogg, for loneliness is a sad thing. Yet they say poverty is more bearable when there are two of you."

"So they say, Madam," said Mr Fogg.

Aouda held out her hand to him. "Then, Mr Fogg, will you have me for your wife?"

Mr Fogg stood up. There was a brightness in his eyes and a tremor on his lips. Then he said simply, "I love you! Yes, indeed, I love you and I am yours!"

Passepartout was called, and appeared at once. Mr Fogg was still holding Aouda's hand in his, and Passepartout immediately understood. His face beamed with delight.

Mr Fogg asked him to go to the Reverend Samuel Wilson's house and arrange for the marriage to take place the next day, Monday. Passepartout ran out of the house.

It was five mintues past eight . . .

14

On the Saturday evening, the five friends of Phileas Fogg were waiting at the Reform Club. Outside, a crowd gathered, for word of the round-the-world journey and the strange bet had been in the newspapers. Many people had taken bets with each other on whether or not the famous Mr Fogg would return in time to win the twenty-thousand pounds. So now, as the hour at which Phileas Fogg was due to arrive drew nearer, the excitement grew.

When the clock inside the Reform Club showed the time as 8.25 pm, Andrew Stuart said, "Gentlemen, Mr Fogg must be here within twenty minutes or he will have lost his bet."

"What time did the last train get in from Liverpool?" asked Thomas Flanagan.

"At 7.23 pm," replied Walter Ralph, "and the next train doesn't get in until ten past twelve."

"If Phileas Fogg had arrived by the seven twenty-three train, he would be here by now," said Andrew Stuart. "So we can take it that we've won our bet."

"We must wait," said Samuel Fallentin. "Mr Fogg never arrives too late or too early, and I wouldn't be at all surprised if he turned up at the last minute."

"If he appears," said Andrew Stuart, who was nervous, "I shan't believe my eyes. The *China* steamer arrived yesterday, and it's the only ship from New York that he could have taken to reach Liverpool in time."

The hands of the clock crept on to 8.40 pm.

"Five more minutes," said Andrew Stuart, anxiously.

They were sitting around a table, trying to play cards, but their eyes kept straying to the clock.

"Eight forty-three," said Thomas Flanagan, cutting the pack.

The room was silent, but outside they could hear the noise of the excited crowd.

"Eight forty-four!" said John Sullivan.

Only one more minute and the bet was won. They stopped playing and began to count the seconds. At the fortieth second, nothing. At the fiftieth, nothing.

At the fifty-fifth second they heard a noise outside like thunder – applause, cheers, all merging into a continuous roar.

The card players rose to their feet.

At the fifty-seventh second the door opened, and before the pendulum had

beaten the sixtieth second, Mr Fogg appeared. He was followed by a large crowd of cheering people.

"Here I am, gentlemen," he said in his usual calm voice.

Yes – Phileas Fogg in person!

What had happened? You will remember that at five past eight in the evening – about twenty-three hours after the travellers arrived in London – Passepartout was sent to the house of the Reverend Samuel Wilson. The clergyman was out so Passepartout waited for twenty minutes.

At 8.35 pm, Passepartout rushed out of the house. He ran as nobody has ever run before, knocking over passers-by and hurtling along the pavement like a tornado! In three minutes he was back at the house in Savile Row where he staggered into Phileas Fogg's room.

He could hardly speak. "Marriage tomorrow . . . impossible . . ."

"Impossible?" said Phileas Fogg. "Why?"

"Because . . . tomorrow . . . is Sunday!"

"Monday," said Mr Fogg.

"No . . . today . . . is Saturday."

"Saturday? Impossible!"

"It is!" cried Passepartout. "You're one day out! We got back *twenty-four hours early* . . . but there's only ten minutes left . . .!"

Passepartout dragged his master out of the house and into a cab, where the driver was promised one hundred pounds if he got to the club in time.

The driver earned his bonus. The clock pointed to 8.45 pm when Phileas Fogg appeared in the morning room. He had gone around the world in eighty days – and he had won his bet of twenty-thousand pounds!

So how could a man as exact, as meticulous as Phileas Fogg have made this error of one day? It was very simple. He had *gained* a day because he had made his journey round the world by travelling towards the east – towards the sun. If he had gone the other way – towards the west – he would have *lost* a day. Passepartout's famous watch – which always showed London time – would have revealed this if, as well as showing the minutes and hours, it had also shown the *days*!

So Phileas Fogg had won twenty thousand pounds. But he had spent nineteen thousand on his journey, and the remaining thousand he shared between Passepartout and the unfortunate Inspector Fix, for Mr Fogg was not a man to bear a grudge. He did, however, deduct the amount of Passepartout's gas bill from his servant's share.

That evening, as dispassionate as ever, he asked Aouda a question. "And will you still marry me?"

"Mr Fogg, it is for me to ask you that question," she replied. "You were ruined and now you are rich . . ."

"That fortune belongs to you," Phileas Fogg told her. "If the idea of marriage had not occurred to you, Passepartout would never have gone to the Reverend Wilson's house and we would never have discovered my mistake, and . . ."

"Dear Mr Fogg," said the young woman.

"Dear Aouda," said Phileas Fogg.

Their marriage took place forty-eight hours later, and Passepartout gave the bride away. Had he not rescued her? Did he not deserve that honour?

Phileas Fogg had completed his journey around the world. He had made use of every means of transport – steamers, railways, carriages, yachts, merchant ships, sledges, elephants – and the eccentric gentleman had remained calm at all times. But what had he gained? What had he brought back from this journey?

Nothing, you may say. Except a charming woman who – however improbable it may seem – was to make him the happiest of men.

And wouldn't anyone travel around the world for that?